Aquatic Grunge

Chris Johnstone

ISBN-13: 978-1463775834

For Sarah

Contents

Chapter One

Chapter Two

Chapter Three

Chapter Four

The Jendaya Chronicle: Part One

Chapter Five

Chapter Six

The Jendaya Chronicle: Part Two

Missives of Merpeople

Chapter Seven

Chapter Eight

Chapter Nine

Missives of Merpeople

Chapter Ten

Chapter Eleven

Stan Dwyer's Night

Nathan Punt's Night

Chapter Twelve

The Jendaya Chronicle: Part Three

Chapter Thirteen

Neville Lives On

Chapter Fourteen

Missives of Merpeople

Chapter Fourteen Continued

The Jendaya Chronicle: Part Four

Chapter Fifteen

Chapter Sixteen

Missives of Merpeople

Chapter Seventeen

Chapter Eighteen

Missives of Merpeople

Chapter Nineteen

Chapter Twenty

Chapter Twenty-One

The Jendaya Chronicle: Part Five

Chapter Twenty-Two

Missives of Merpeople

Chapter Twenty-Three

Missives of Merpeople: Final Missive

Chapter One

I lived in a cheap backpackers hostel in Cairns. There was nothing wrong with communal living. Actually, the bunks in the dorm of the Paradise Hostel, on Grafton Street, weren't too bad—not as good as the name suggests, but not too bad. I had an arrangement with the manager: mop the floors, clean the toilets, do various other unglamorous jobs; and stay rent-free. The manager was a short and wide sort of bloke called Steve. Steve never hesitated to put me to work and I was starting to wonder if the hard labour was worth the twenty eight dollars I was saving each night.

One Thursday morning, as I was mopping the communal kitchen, I scanned the area. It's amazing how you can look at a place for ages, months, without even really looking at it. Brown floor tiles, brown walls and a brown ceiling. Resident geckos crawled along the walls, standing out like green glow-sticks at a rave. Despite their luster, the moths usually didn't see them until it was much too late. There was a massive brown fridge taking up a whole wall. It had four big glass doors and a shit-load of shelves. It was pretty much known that if you put something in there, there was a good chance that you would never see it again. I had a thought of a mature-aged man placing his moaning battle-axe of a wife in the fridge in hope. An A4-size piece of paper was stuck up on the glass. Written in bold purple marker pen was the following note: 'Please don't steal from others. Karma, guys. Karma.'

'Jeez, that's a bit rough,' I thought. 'I was just about to help myself to somebody's Kraft Cheese Singles, but fuck, I hadn't realised that karma would be onto me.'

I leaned against my mop for a while, pondering. After eight minutes, I figured that karma would want to reward me for my hard work in the kitchen, so I grabbed a handful of stuffed green olives, straight out of a jar. Someone had left the jar in a very vulnerable position close to the front and in plain view of everyone. It would have been rude not to take them.

Hmm, I was getting thirsty. What to wash those karmalicious olives down with? And then I spotted it—the find of the century. Some brave (or stupid) soul had bought a slab of VB Gold and stuffed it in the top left-hand corner of the fridge. It was literally a chest of gold in front of me.

Who would leave an unguarded slab? Bring it on!

I approached it stealthily, making sure that it was not a trap. He or she had tried their best to hide it behind several browning heads of lettuce and a packet of vacuum-sealed bacon. But my eyes were trained to look beyond these things. As I reached for the Holy Grail, I saw a Post-it note stuck to the side of the cardboard box that read: Two of the bottles in this box have been stuck up my arse. Only I am knowing which ones they are. How are you liking those odds? Horst.

Which way will karma go? There was only one way to tell. I checked the time. Eleven a.m. I grabbed the whole box and headed for my room, hoping to consume all but the two arse-beers before anybody noticed. I slammed the door shut and quickly opened a stubby. I heard the satisfying 'sttsss,' of the twist top coming off. As I put sweet beer to chapped lips, I was rudely interrupted.

'You know what the bleeding time is, guv?'

'Oh, shit, sorry. Didn't see you there.'

The pile of whitish sheets and pillows on the bunk bed opposite me had wakened, taking the form of a whitish pom called Neville. We had been sharing the dorm for three weeks. In the world of backpacking, that made us best friends.

His presence made me apprehensive, not because I was busted, but because I was most likely going to have to share my hard-earned bounty with him.

'What's this then, 'ey?' he demanded. 'Go on, offer us one.'

'I can't,' I mumbled. 'These belong to Horst.'

'Well maybe I'll go ask 'im if I can 'ave one — know what I mean?' he threatened.

'No need to do that, mate,' I said. 'I'd love to have a couple of quiet ones with you. Can you do me one favour, though?'

'What's that then, guv?' He enquired, as he grabbed a stubby from the box.

'Fuck off back to your own country!'

He wasn't a bad bloke, but his red hair, bony limbs, pasty complexion, and pure pomminess were just asking for insults.

We drank. I made sure to check each stubby for any signs of German rectum before deciding which one was for me and which one was for Neville. After a while though, I wouldn't have cared if the beer was flowing direct to my mouth from Boris Becker's ginger-lined arsehole.

After about eight beers and endless hours of Neville crapping on about shagging, drinking, and the 2002 Rugby World Cup final, I fell asleep. I dreamt mainly about drinking beer, good quality beer that I had paid for myself.

When I woke up, I checked my watch. It was six o'clock, but I couldn't tell whether that meant a.m. or p.m. During summer, Cairns only knew one way — hot and humid. Morning, night, or afternoon, it didn't matter. It really couldn't be too difficult for the local Cairns weatherman. In fact, I reckoned I could do a better job than him:

Kelvin Daniels here. Today folks, it's going to be unbearably sticky and hot. That will pretty much continue the whole day, the whole night, and continue in this pattern for fucking months. I'd suggest immersing yourself in water and getting shit-faced until May. Now, it's back to the anchor-man, who wasn't good enough to stay on-air in a capital city, so he's stuck in Cairns pretending he is happy to be here, like the rest of us stuck in this backward shit-hole where bogans and back-packers roam free.

At six o'clock, morning or night, Neville was not around. I could hear some masculine cursing in the background. I couldn't understand it, but it sounded pretty German.

I'd been living in the hostel for nearly two months. I was an elder statesman of the place. People from all over the world came and went all the time. I wasn't too worried about Horst, as yet unknown to me. Chances were he'd be gone in a couple of days.

My decision to live communally was based on sex. I figured if you are living side-by-side and sleeping in dorms with backpackers from all over the world, statistics predict that half of them are going to be women. These women would be forced to talk to me if they lived with me, and some of them might even find me attractive. That was the concept. However, most of the women saw me for what I was: a loner; a useless bludger who used travelling as a way of hiding the fact that I had no prospects, no future, no friends, and no fucking idea. Not that you could call going to Cairns from Melbourne 'travelling'. I was still in the same bloody country. In the two months I'd been in Cairns, I'd had sex twice—yes, with two separate women, but that's still not a great strike rate, especially in Cairns. Both encounters involved masses of money spent on alcohol for me and the chicks I was conning into bed. Both women wanted nothing to do with me ever again. I don't blame them.

You don't have to have any special qualities to travel. In fact, you don't need to have any good traits at all. Most of the backpackers at the hostel were worse than me: boring, self-centred, and fairly humourless until drunk or stoned. They were all, like me, alcoholics.

Judging by the fact that I could hear voices that weren't too loud and drunk, I guessed it must be six at night. I wasn't sure what to do. I decided I should skull the remaining five beers and dispose of them under Neville's bed. I then heard a voice, or had an internal awakening. Whatever it was, it asked this in a cold, masculine voice:

'What the hell are you going to do with your life, mate?'

'I don't know. Drink?' I replied.

'That's not really much of a goal, now is it?'

'I guess not. But it is achievable,' I countered.

'You are better than that. Hurry up and do something,' the voice demanded, 'the time has come, Kelvin Daniels, the time has come!'

'You are right, mysterious voice, you are absolutely right!' I screamed, possibly way too loud.

I resolved then and there to get a job, a title, a life, and some respect. And there was no time like tomorrow. That night, however, I celebrated my new determination and focus by going out and getting absolutely smashed.

Chapter Two

My head was pounding. My body was aching. I moved my head and opened my eyes, scanning my surroundings. There were four bunk beds and a poster of Godzilla on the wall. Right place—TICK. There was no evidence to suggest I had vomited, shat or pissed on my property or myself. Important TICK for communal living. There was nobody next to me in my bed—TICK (especially going on my record of what I find attractive after a few drinks). I could see my mobile phone, keys and wallet all neatly flung in the corner on the floor. Bonus TICK.

The walls were spinning like the firesticks of a crazed hippy. Crazed hippy? That rang a bell. My recollections of the previous night were still fairly vague. I know I was drunk when I got to the Woolshed at about seven. I'm sure the big Maori bouncer only just let me in. I ate a plate of fettuccine. Staying at the Paradise Hostel entitled us to a free, but pretty small, meal every night. The carbs I ingested could not soak up all of the alcohol, as was my plan. For dessert, I had tequila slammers with some lads from the hostel. I recalled:

Robert Palmer's Simply Irresistible.

Alcohol.

Crawling around on damp grass.

Laughter.

That's all I could think of at the time and I dozed off again. The next time I woke up I checked my watch and saw that it was eight o'clock. Pretending to myself that I would get up to clean the toilets before nine, I crashed out again. As I was dozing off, I imagined I was riding a flying unicorn into the pink clouds of heaven—a heaven with chocolate and sex and without cleaning and work.

I woke up again at about two p.m. Fuck. As I was trying to formulate some sort of bullshit excuse that Steve wouldn't believe, the top bunk opposite me started to move around. This was the bed that had always been empty as long as I'd known it.

The person in it was a big broad guy. He had a shock of brown hair, brown eyes, and tanned, brown skin. He was the antithesis of Neville, who lay unmoving in the bunk below him. Brown-man looked at me and smiled.

'Kelvin, mate,' said Mr God-Knows-Who-You-Are. 'How'd you pull up, buddy?' His Cairns accent was as broad and tanned as he was.

'Not bad,' I lied.

I was at that point unsuccessfully trying to insert this person into any memory of mine at all. It struck me that I must have met this guy last night. Fuck, I hope I didn't have sex with him.

'Yourself, mate?' It was the best I could do.

'Yeah, sweet, mate, sweet. I'm stoked we steered clear of that trouble last night, ay?' he said.

There was a long pause.

'But thanks for letting us crash here for the night. I don't think I coulda made it back to Trinity Wharf in my state, ay?'

Silence. Man, my head hurt.

'Yeah,' I finally said.

The burly, brown guy jumped down from the bunk bed. Neville let out a little cockney snore.

'What trouble was that again, mate?' I asked, trying to sound as if I actually knew what the fuck he was talking about.

'Oh, yeah. Youse were pretty smashed, ay?'

'Yeah, I can't remember much.'

'Well, mate, we'd left the Woolshed and were trying to get back here. I was following youse guys. There was a whole bunch of us. Nobody really seemed to know how to get home though. Somehow we found ourselves on the boulevard, near that big swimming pool, ay?'

'Yeah.'

'There was a bunch of hippies playing their bongos or something, and youse all were dancing to it like a bunch of poofters. Youse were really getting into it, mate. Youse were so into it that you fell over and crashed into a guy with dreadlocks who was meditating or something, ay?'

'Oh yeah, now I remember,' I lied.

'Well these hippies went sick and started swinging at everybody. That's probably how you got that bruise on your face, ay?'

I felt my left cheek. Ow!

'I was in the background for most of this, so I sorta' charged them and they shat themselves and left us alone, ay?'

'Yeah, thanks for that.'

'Don't worry, mate, you thanked me enough last night. Youse kept on going, 'Stan, youse are my saviour and best friend in the world' and stuff, ay?'

'Yeah.'

North Queenslanders have a different way of talking. They speak in a slow, lazy drawl. It takes them ages to say anything. Once they get to the end of their sentence, they tack 'ay?' at the end of it. It turns everything they say into a question. A statement such as, 'It's a full moon,' does not require a response. But 'It's a full moon out there, ay?' does. It makes it impossible to end a conversation because they keep asking fucking questions every time they talk. Stan's 'ay' was the counterpoint to Neville's 'innit?' East-enders had their own way of not ending a conversation.

I had a brief notion of the two of them locked in an endless exchange:

'Good, innit?'

'Yeah, ay?'

'Good, innit?'

'Yeah, ay?'

'Good, innit?'

'Yeah, ay?'

And so on, tanned versus white, until one of them died.

'I should head. But if youse are still interested in that job we were talking about, give us a call. The boat leaves in about two weeks. If you get your open water before then, it should be sweet.'

'I'll just get your mobile number, mate.'

'You've already got it, ay? Check your phone. Give us a call soon so we can book you in for the course, ay?'

Stan bounded from the room energetically. Job? See, getting drunk does get results.

Stan's standing spot was replaced by Steve within minutes. He was standing in as broad-shouldered a manner as possible: he must have thought that the extra two centimetres of width made him no longer fat, short, or bald. When he stood like that, you knew that he was pissed off with an underling or a customer.

'I want you out of here within the fortnight.'

His shoulders told me there wasn't going to be a way out of it this time.

'Okay.'

He reacted with annoyance. He'd obviously prepared a speech based on my questioning his reasoning. When I plainly accepted his proposal, he was confused and even angrier. He decided to plough ahead with his strategy, regardless.

'Your work is rubbish. You steal food and alcohol from the fridge. You never wake up on time. You are just shit, and it's time for you to move on.'

'But I've got two weeks, right?'

'Yeah, as your landlord I am obliged by law to not kick your sorry arse out for two weeks. In the '80s, we would have just run you out of here.'

'Okay.'

I wanted to scream at him that nobody cares about the '80s and its occupancy laws. I wanted to tell him that he looked like a special-needs shelf-packer in his shorts, polo shirt, sandals and comb-over. But I knew that the best thing to do was nothing. And he was right. I was shit.

He stood there lingering, prepared for battle. I slept.

Chapter Three

'All right, Neville. I need to get a job. This guy told me that I could get a job if I get my 'open water'. Do you know what that is?'

'Well, it's like this, guv,' replied the lairy geezer. 'When a woman is about to give birth, right, she gets what is known as her 'open water,' right? That's when you know when to zip her off to the 'ospital quick-smart, innit? My mother got her 'open water' four minutes before I shot out. The ambulance 'adn't even got out of the driveway.'

He laughed in an uncontrolled, high-pitched squeal. He clearly appreciated his own humour. I left him to it.

Now that I was sure that I was not welcome at the hostel, I could be much more blatant about stealing food and not doing any work. I headed to the kitchen, thinking greedy thoughts of forbidden two-minute noodles.

A ringing sound came out of my shorts. I jumped. People rarely phone me.

'G'day, this is Stan here, ay?'

'Hey, Stan, it's Kelvin Daniels here.'

'Orright, Kelvin mate,' he drawled. 'Are youse still up for working?'

'Yeah, man, like we said. I'd be good at it.'

'The boss wants to have a gander at youse before he lets youse on the boat, ay? No wuckers?' He asked, sounding like he was doing an over-the-top impression of an Australian.

'That is perfectly understandable,' I replied in my best Queen's English.

'Grouse. There's another job garn if youse know anyone's up for it,'

'I must apologise, I didn't quite understand that last statement.'

My posh accent was obviously starting to get on his tits. He repeated himself loudly and slowly.

'I said, IF YOUSE KNOW ANY OTHER DIVER, COOJA BRING 'EM ALONG, COS THERE'S ANOTHER JOB GARN! You're a mouthy little tripper, ay?'

'Oh, do forgive me. If any offense was caused, I most sincerely assure you the intention of aggravation was completely absent from my disposition,' I said, causing Stan to pause for a while.

After fifteen seconds: 'So do youse know anyone? We don't wanna' be a bloke short. The Skip's got some good spots in mind. We're gonna' haul up some slug.'

'Yeah, maybe. I'll see.'

Haul up some slug?

'I'll text the address to youse. He wants to see youse today. Bring that maybe-guy along with ya, ay?'

End communication.

Boat? Haul up some slug? Hmmm. Was this a gay swinger's party boat? Would the captain ask me to strip before employing me? What if they asked me to haul up my slug first?

I pictured the captain greeting me at the door wearing only an admiral's hat, a leather G-string and a mischievous grin, hidden underneath his thick, black moustache: 'Hi there, sailor boy. Wanna' sink my battleship?'

I needed back-up at that meeting. There was no way I was going to confront the situation by myself. So I gritted my teeth and did the unthinkable.

He was standing in the swimming pool, his skinny, white chest gleaming. He was singing the tune of 'Land of hope and glory,' but had replaced the lyrics with his description of Jonny Wilkinson scoring a try for England. It killed me to do it.

'Neville, mate. Are you interested in working with me?'

'Fecking 'ell, geezer, I've been waiting for you to ask. No worries. What's the biz, then?'

'Well, I don't know what the job involves at all. All I know is that the boss wants to meet us. We've got to go see him now.'

I checked the text message on my phone. It read: BECHE DE MER DIVING. 168 DIGGER STREET. ARKSE FOR JESSE BARNES AT THE FRONT DESK. YOUSE CAN SAY STAN SENT YOU AND OTHER MAYBE GUY, AY?

Wow! He actually texted like he talked.

Neville and I hastily smoked a joint and then started the short walk down Grafton Street. Grafton Street eventually turned into Digger Street, getting uglier the further you got away from the centre of town, the 'city.'

The joint did the opposite of calming me down; it made me more paranoid than a goat at a lions' convention. This gig was getting scarier with every step we took along Digger Street.

It was time to calm down and go inside. At the front of 168 Digger Street, a white sign told us to ring the doorbell for any inquiries to Beche De Mer Diving. As we approached the door, a small ball of hair and fury came hurtling towards us.

'Arf, arf, arf, arf, arf, arf, arf, arf, arf!'

It stopped two feet in front of us, bared its teeth and let out a low, guttural, 'Grrrrrrrrrrr.'

Before I had time to decide what to do it ran back to wherever it came from. Neville returned from behind a tree.

After composing myself, I went to ring the doorbell. The front door swung open before I had a chance. I was welcomed by the sight of a young woman. She had wavy, blonde hair and deep, green eyes that matched her polo shirt. Her body was slight, but in proportion, and her brown cords and bare feet gave her the 'cool-without-trying' look that most people spend heaps on. All in all, I was starting to think that maybe this boat wasn't such a bad idea.

I smiled.

'You must be Jesse Barnes.'

'No,' she suppressed a laugh. 'My name is Victoria. Sorry about Harlot before; she's very protective. Just wait here, and I'll get Jesse for you.'

While we were waiting, Neville blurted out what I had been thinking.

'Not 'alf bad, innit? Would not mind jamming that under the covers, know what I mean?'

Ignoring Neville, I tried to picture Jesse Barnes in my mind. He had morphed into an attractive, red-headed woman with huge tits. She was Victoria's sometime girlfriend, who liked to screw the new crew.

A large man with a large stomach came to the door.

'G'day, Jesse Barnes.' He didn't offer his hand. 'This way, boys.'

Damn. His hairy arse-crack led us into his office.

'So how's it going?'

'Good,' we replied in unison.

'Good. I'll tell you about this next trip and what I need you two to do for me,' he declared in a strong, gruff voice.

As he was talking, I noticed the walls of his office. It was full of shark jaws, the type I've seen mounted in the same way on the walls of pubs before. He had at least twenty of them. Occupying the rest of the wall space were photos of himself next to large, dead fish. He was pictured smiling next to limp, hanging sharks and strung-up marlins. He had the same slumped posture and proud moustachioed grin in all of them. There was one of him next to a gigantic green fish, its expression bemused.

' ...is pretty important to remember. So, is that clear, boys?'

Paying attention has never been a strong point of mine.

'Yes,' we chorused, Neville more confidently than me.

'All right, then. So I've got an account with Specialised Divers. We can take the cost of the 'open water' off your earnings from the first trip. I'll get Victoria to text you the details. After that, you boys will be ready to come out to sea with the crew. Any questions?'

'No.'

We made for the door.

'And, Daniels,' he bellowed with a smile in his voice.

'Yeah,' I said as I was nearly out of the office.

'I've heard you're a bit of a mouthy cunt. Fucking watch it!'

Chapter Four

There were six people doing the diving course. We had been ushered into a small classroom by a woman with too much makeup on. The six of us made polite conversation and laughed at things that really weren't that funny in order to stop any awkward silences.

The group was comprised of myself, Neville, Rod (a middle-aged, middle-weight American man) and three backpackers from Switzerland. They introduced themselves as Heidi, Margrit, and Crispin. The Swiss trio were travelling together.

Neville took the floor.

'So this is Kelvin, innit? Me and 'im are going to be sea cucumber divers in two-week's time. We're gonna crawl on the bottom of the ocean and pick up the little blighters.'

'Really?' said American Rod. 'Who buys them?'

'They're shipped off to Asia, mainly,' I said.

And that, apparently, was true. I wasn't concentrating when Jesse was talking to us, but Neville swore he wasn't lying when he told me what we were doing.

A man walked in. He was a man with presence.

His broad shoulders held up his huge, barrel chest. He had crystal-blue eyes, which were complemented by the blue Specialised Divers polo-top he was wearing. His blond hair was short enough to be neat, but long enough to be a little bit wavy and crazy. Margrit and Heidi were impressed. So was I.

'Hello, guys, my name is Warren,' he said. 'I'll be your dive instructor for the duration of this course.'

He was tanned, buff, relaxed and in control.

'First, we are going to do some theory sessions before we hop into the swimming pool. During this time, if you have any questions or queries, just yell out. You don't have to put your hand up. We are all adults here.' As he finished his sentence, he glanced towards Neville. The rest of the group snickered. Heidi and Margrit looked Warren up and down more thoroughly than I had been.

Soon after, we all had to start focusing our minds on different matters.

It had been a rare mistake of Warren's to advise us to ask questions willy-nilly. Rod took it as a direct order to cut in with inane bullshit whenever Warren paused to take a breath. Here is a highlights package of the rest of Rod's performance throughout the sixty-seven long minutes we were in the classroom together, all of it delivered in a whiny, oh-so-friendly American accent. We'll start at the five minutes and thirty-two second mark.

'Tell me, Warren, what kind of fish do you have in Australia? In Florida, we have bass, catfish, and pickerel. They are all freshwater fish. We also have a big problem with carp and walking catfish. That's right, walking catfish. They are both introduced species. Do you get much of that 'down under,' Warren?'

7:12: 'So, what do you do if you get taken by a shark? I mean, in Florida we have gators, but at least we know where they are. It's not like you'll come across a White Pointer sunning itself on a golf course. Am I right, guys?'

16:05: 'How about this heat?'

26:35: 'I guess the unicorn could have used some scuba equipment when he missed Noah's ark. Huh, guys?'

38:01: 'So, what are the chances of us being in the water when a tsunami hits? I'd want to be pretty deep in the water when that happens.'

43:58: 'Boy, this heat is intense. I've been to Egypt, South Africa, and Nepal, but this tops it by a mile.'

54:12: 'So, what's with coral?'

56:08: 'Hey, we could probably find Nemo out there. How about that?'

65:05: 'Boy, this sure is taking a while. I feel like we've been sitting here for ages. I just can't wait to stop talking and start diving. What about you guys?'

Finally, the gruelling classroom session ended. It was a credit to Warren's patience that he didn't punch Rod's head in, while explaining to him why the world would be a better place with him dead. Despite the constant distraction, he explained everything to us firmly, without being aggressive. Occasionally he threw in a reliable, well-worn joke. He answered all of Rod's queries with patience and humour. Most importantly, he educated us at a level that I could comprehend. Tens of minutes later, I could still recall the things he had taught me.

He explained that you have to pop your ears, or 'equalise' every metre or so that you go down in the water or your eardrums would cave in. He also explained a bunch of other shit that I got the gist of before we hit the pool.

The first thing we had to do was change into our bathers. In a completely non-homosexual way, I quickly surveyed the other guys' naked bodies in the change-room. They were all pretty average, like me.

As Rod was getting changed, he kept talking to me. He kept crapping on about Florida, even when he was completely naked. I thought that Neville was annoying, but Rod easily had him covered. When he asked me a question about Melbourne, I went to answer and was greeted with his hairy, arse-crack staring right back at me. How fucking rude!

As commonly happens, the girls took longer to get changed than the guys. The delay, I hoped, was caused by their talking about how much they liked me, while fondling each other's breasts. As Margrit and Heidi finally emerged from the change-rooms, it was obvious that Rod, Neville, Warren, Crispin and I were all checking them out—big time.

They were both pretty, by any standards, of which I have none. The Swiss Miss duo giggled and spoke Swiss words to each other as they climbed into the pool. Margrit had short, auburn hair. Her skin was tanned. She was slim and taller than me. Heidi was blonde, smaller and curvier than Margrit. They both wore black string bikinis that barely covered their breasts. As I was surveying their entry into the shallow end of the pool, I had to inconspicuously fashion my erection so it was pointing skyward. If anyone had looked at me closely, they would have been able to see the smallest amount of head peering up from the elastic of my shorts.

'Wouldn't mind munching on a double-Swiss cheeseburger,' whispered Neville, from a safe distance.

'That would go down nicely with a beer, Neville,' I replied.

After that we had to tread water for ten minutes, just to show we were comfortable in the water. If we couldn't do it, we were refunded and shown the door. I suspect we all hoped that Rod would drown, or at least fail.

'Excuse me, Warren,' he said, as Warren braced himself for the inevitable. 'Does that mean that we can use another person as a flotation device?'

'No,' said Warren, acting a laugh.

'No worries, pal. Another thing—' Rod continued, but was suddenly cut off.

'I am not such a good swimmer,' said Crispin in a deep, commanding European voice. 'I need to be concentrating and I need you to be shutting the fuck up. You understand, yes?'

That had been the first thing the man had said all day.

'Yeah, no worries buddy,' was Rod's sheepish reply.

For the next 600 seconds, the six of us trod water in complete, beautiful silence. If Rod looked like he was about to talk, he was met with a solid glare from the Swiss man and that was the end of it.

We spent hours in the pool, going through different skills and exercises. Even Rod realised that he was out of his natural element, so he decided to shut up and actually listen. Using the equipment was fun and I was actually quite good at it. Already I could control my buoyancy using the air in my lungs or by putting air into my buoyancy vest. I could take my mask off, put it back on, and clear the water out of it. I could take my regulator out of my mouth and put it back in.

And all of that I could do while under water. I was a gun. I was born to dive.

I sucked up to Warren like a teacher's pet. Whenever he needed a volunteer, I put my hand up. I was always the first to attempt a new skill and was always first to master anything we were given. He seemed to take an interest in me. We chatted while the rest of the crew were still trying to master some of the skills that were piss-easy to me.

'So, tell us mate, what brought you to Cairns?' he asked.

'I came up here to learn how to dive,' I replied.

I am not a very talented man, but I am an above average liar. I feel more comfortable when I'm talking absolute bullshit. Being truthful is pretty boring and often hurtful.

'Yeah, I've always been interested in fish and the ocean. I really wanted to see all of it up close,' I fibbed.

'Well, that's good, mate. You should look into getting some dives up, and working with us or one of the other dive operators.'

'How do you do that?'

'Well, once you've got enough dives logged, it's just a matter of doing the training courses, mate. It takes a bit of work, but you can get up to instructor standard fairly quickly. You've just got to do the hundred or so dives, and you're set.'

'Well I've never been afraid of hard work,' I lied again.

Everyone else had, by then, come to the surface. He paused before addressing the whole group in his commanding-yet-friendly voice.

'Now, guys, that was really good. I'll give you a bit of free time to practice anything and everything that we have been through today, before we hop out of the pool. Neville, you need to keep practicing mask removal and replacement.'

'Look, guv, I know what you're saying, but the chlorine keeps getting in my eyes. It's not that I'm in pain or nuffin, it's just that my eyes are my sexiest feature, and I don't want to be disappointin' the ladies, innit?'

The Jendaya Chronicle: Part One

My brothers, my mummy, my daddy and I used to live in Zimbabwe. For a while, it was good. My mummy and my daddy loved me very much. They probably still do love me, from wherever they are.

The childhood that I can remember was fun. I played with my identical twin brothers all the time when we were really little. I looked after them when they were at school. It helped that my mummy was a teacher at my school. Nobody picked on us, and we had lots of friends.

Jabulani and Emmanuel (my brothers) were two years younger than me and I loved them very much. Jabi was much braver and bolder than Emmi. Emmi was more thoughtful and relaxed than Jabi. I was somewhere in between, which came in handy if I was needed to resolve a disagreement between them. I could tell them apart by the way they walked, talked and just were. They both had fine black hair and deep brown eyes. They loved each other, and they also loved Mummy, Daddy and me.

The longer that time goes by, the less I can remember of the school, my brothers, my mummy and my daddy. Daddy had blond hair and blue eyes. Mummy looked more like most of the people in Zimbabwe.

Daddy was a farmer. Every day, he would get up really early in the morning and start farming. Mummy, Emmi, Jabi and I would help him out on the weekends and after school. Daddy never made us get up as early in the morning as he did. We would usually eat bota for breakfast. It was quite plain, but it filled me up for a long time. Mummy had a garden with lots of plants, where she grew fruit and vegetables. We often had tomatoes, zucchini and lettuce from the garden. We would sometimes eat it with our sadza for dinner. Once, for the twins' twelfth birthday, we cooked two of our chickens. The chickens were my friends and I was sad when Daddy killed them, but he explained to me that it was an honourable death for them. They had stopped laying eggs, and it was time for them to go back into the magical circle of energy. I stopped worrying. They tasted delicious. I'd never eaten chicken before, and I haven't since.

One afternoon, after we'd walked home from school, Daddy was gone. Mummy told us that he went on a holiday and that we would see him soon.

The next day some men with guns visited Mummy. They spoke for a long time. I didn't know what they were talking about. The men left in their big green car very shortly after they had arrived. Mummy went quiet for the rest of the night.

The morning after, Mummy said she needed for Jabi, Emmi and I to help her pack up our things. She said that we were going on a holiday. We were excited and helped as quickly as we could. We were hurried along by Mummy. We put all of our things into the car and we drove off after bedtime. Mummy didn't tell us where we were going.

Chapter Five

I stood alone, studying Marlin Wharf and all of the boats coming in and out. There were hundreds of them, some small and some large. Even a massive grey Navy vessel cruised past. I had to concentrate on the boats. Rod was lurking around with intent and there was no way I was going to get caught in his web of talk.

Our time in the swimming pool had flown by. By the end of day two, we all knew how to set up our dive gear, and we all pretty much knew how to use it properly.

We hadn't ventured anywhere near the open ocean, which is what we were going to do as soon as the Specialised Diver boat arrived.

Marlin Wharf worked like a busy car park at Woolworths, except in slow motion. One massive boat got untied and left its parking space, and the next moment another massive boat would park itself in the vacant spot. Masses of tourists were embarking and disembarking. They were mainly Asians. About half of the people that were boarding the Specialised Diver were Asian too. I've never shagged an Asian bird; I wouldn't mind it though.

My thought process was broken by Neville's unmistakeable voice in the distance. He was talking to the Swiss girls.

'So, I says, "Guv, 'ow was I supposed to know that was your pint? I didn't see your name on it!" And then, the bastard kicked me square in the bollocks. It bleedin' well 'urt.'

As he said this, he put both hands over his groin and started grimacing, reliving the moment.

Margrit and Heidi stayed silent and looked at each other, not knowing what to say or do.

Amongst all the traffic and activity that was Marlin Wharf, suddenly there was an abrupt awkward silence.

'True story, that,' Neville mumbled to himself, looking at the ground.

In the distance, I could see the Specialised Diver coming our way. The boat would soon be ready for boarding. None of us could wait to get on it, or at the very least, get away from that silence.

As we embarked the big white cruiser, I made a special effort to try to remain close to Margrit and Heidi. My plan worked, because when they chose a place to sit down, I was able to 'accidentally' sit opposite them in the same booth. The booths fit four people, leaving one spot vacant. I placed my backpack on the empty seat, hoping any would-be takers could take the hint and fuck off.

Not so, because along came Rod—the greying man with the greying personality—and sat right down next to me, handing me my bag.

'So, this is pretty neato, huh guys?'

The three of us muttered agreement, and looked out of the window towards the sea. The boat had started moving, and the ocean started flying beneath us. However, my plan of working my certain brand of magic on the Swiss girls was being snuffed out by 'Hot-Rod' next to me. He wouldn't let up. Occasionally he would ask the group a question, but it was purely to allow him to talk more about himself.

'So, guys, have you seen any musical acts out here lately?' He asked.

To which Margrit replied, 'Yes, we saw British India at The Corner Hotel in Melbourne.'

'It was really rocking,' chipped in Heidi.

'You've been to The Corner?' I asked, sensing an opening. 'That used to be one of my old watering holes. What's British India's live show like? I haven't seen them yet.'

Rod could feel control slipping away from him. He made his move.

'I was talking about real rock and roll. Bands like The Grateful Dead, Toto, and Genesis. You know, I once saw ELO when they last toured the States. I even got the autograph of Kelly Groucutt.'

Opening closed.

'He's their bass player. He has a remarkable falsetto voice, and his backing vocals intertwine with Jeff Lynne's voice real well. It makes for a totally neato show.'

And on and on he went. I was starting to feel sick. I wasn't sure if it was because I had been sober for two days straight, or whether it was because that fuckwitted, symbol-of-the-free-West imbecile was sitting next to me. Whatever the reason, I felt real crook and it hit me real quick.

'So cross-country skiing is for real men, whereas snowboarding is for people who like to show off. I'm a real man, so I like to—hey, hey!'

'Blloooorghghgh!'

I threw up all over him. I'm still not sure if I aimed at him or not. I didn't have much choice: it was either Rod, or all over the table. So, Rod copped it thick and hard. I had eaten Hungry Jacks on the way to the boat, and had upgraded the meal, so there was a man-sized feast of partially digested onion rings, Coca Cola, and beef burger all over Rod's white shirt and grey trousers.

I went to apologise.

'Blloooorghghgh!'

The girls ran from the cubicle, without a drop on them. I was pretty clean too, for that matter. There were just a few flecks in my hair and on my Hawaiian shirt. Rod was a different story; one movement from him, and my reincarnated brunch would fly everywhere.

I leaped over him, making for the toilets, as quickly as I could, leaving Rod where he was. He was a pile of orange crap with eyes.

I spent the remainder of the trip worshipping the porcelain God. I wretched and munted for fucking hours, until the boat started slowing down and the ocean became calm again.

Neville gave me the rundown on what happened to Rod after I'd pasted him.

'Well, he sorta' just sat there in silence for a while, which is fecking unusual for starters, know what I mean? The two lasses went and got Wazza (Warren), who brought a rubbish bin wiv 'im. Wazza told that Yanky twat to take his clothes off carefully. 'E somehow managed to get his kit off wiffout spilling any of your precious vomitus anywhere. Twas fucking brilliant. Now, Rod's wearing a Specialised Divers polo shirt like the rest of them geezers. He's strutting round like he's shit-hot.'

'Oh, so everything worked out all right, then?' I asked.

'Look, guv, you're not the most popular lad on the boat, and I wouldn't pin your 'opes on either of the Swiss misses. But, yeah, it's all been taken care of, and the place doesn't even smell that bad.'

Soon it was time to gear up and get ready for our first dive. I had to clear my mind and try to remember all of the stuff we'd gone over in the last two days. It was as if all of the knowledge I'd acquired had been forced out of my mouth and nostrils, along with the mucus, bile and stomach-lining.

Warren systematically marched from person to person, making sure that our air was turned on, weight-belts secure, masks were spat in and washed clean, fins were on, and minds focused. The man was reassuring and encouraging, especially with the two ladies.

I was shitting myself—not literally, which was lucky. One outburst from one orifice a day is enough.

Warren gathered the six of us together on the back deck for a predive pep talk.

'Okay, guys, we are about to head in. I've seen you all do your buddy checks and I've checked everything too. We are all going to have a great dive.'

The weather was hot, humid and unforgiving. The tight, rubber wetsuit was making me sweat. I looked over at my dive buddy. Neville was not a creature in his natural element. His normally beady eyes were magnified by his dive mask. His long, plastic snorkel dangled on the side of his face like some sort of prosthetic penis (well, he was a dickhead). It was obvious that his weight belt, buoyancy jacket and the clunky air tank on his back weighed him down. The fact that he was attempting to walk around in fins—similar in size to Krusty the Clown's shoes—didn't help his already restricted mobility. He was perspiring profusely and looked scared.

I felt and looked just as ridiculous as he did and I was thinking about pulling out when I heard the call.

'All right, boys, you're up,' said Warren.

'No worries then, guv,' said Neville.

Neville pushed ahead of me, without even a sideways glance. He shuffled his body to the side of the boat, waiting on the edge, where he was about to jump in. He put his regulator in his mouth and stepped forward purposefully, his hand over his face.

Splish. He was in and paddling out to the rest of the group, who were floating on the surface. I followed his lead, and pretty soon after that we were under the water.

Fucking awesome!

There was fucking everything down there. There were small colourful fish, massive silver fish, small silver fish, and massive colourful fish. There were lots of fucking fish, and man, they were fucking everywhere.

Once under the water, I instantly forgot about the preceding embarrassment back on the boat. I pretty much forgot about all of my troubles among the terrestrial population. All that mattered was that I was flying through the water, weightless and fancy-free. I was a superhero, surveying a strange new planet, trying to gauge if the weird inhabitants were as friendly as they seemed.

There was this huge, green fish that was roughly the size and weight of Steve, but it had much more joie de vivre. The emerald giant followed the group around, always keeping a safe distance. It acted like a child in primary school who was trying to be part of the cool gang, but didn't want to let on. Once, it cruised close enough to me that I could see intricate patterns on the side of its body. It looked like a henna artist had gone to town on it, except no human could come up with designs that subtle and beautiful. Warren told me later that it was called 'Wally,' and that most dive sites in Far North Queensland had a resident Wally. I recognised it from one of the photos in Jesse Barnes' office, strung up like a free-thinking martyr.

Chapter Six

'That was well-wicked, that was.'

'Yeah, I guess it was all right, mate,' I replied.

I tried to act cool about it for some unknown reason. It was better than all right; it was the most awesome thing I had experienced in my life. We were back on board, changed and ready for drinks. Neville and I told ourselves that we needed to calm our nerves after such an awe-inspiring awakening, but the fact was, as always, we simply wanted alcohol.

I like alcohol.

One of the best things about the boat was the honesty system they had in place. It was up to us to mark a line next to our name every time we took an item from the fridge. These two beers were courtesy of Chung Ho, an as-yet-unmet fellow scuba diver.

'Cheers, guv,' said Neville, as we cracked open our first VB.

'Cheers, Chung!'

'Yeah, right. Guv, how good a gig would it be to work on this boat?'

'Mate, it would be all right.'

Neville had a point. The boat had shaggable women on it. I didn't rate my chances, because I wasn't one of the dive instructors. The ladies were always around Warren and his cronies, laughing at their jokes and touching their tanned arms. It was a good lifestyle they had there. The thought of diving into an ocean paradise by day, and diving into foreign pussy by night, was appealing.

Neville and I had another VB, and another. Chung was a fucking generous benefactor, God bless him.

'So, guv, I reckon that the biggest twat going round is....'

Neville got up mid-sentence and left. The reason became apparent.

'Hey there, pal. Are you feeling better?'

It was Rod. I had managed to avoid talking to him since the vomit incident.

'Yeah, mate. I'm really sorry about before. I really didn't mean it,' I said.

'Don't worry about it, pal,' he said, as he put two frosty VBs on the table.

'Here, I got you a beer to show you there are no hard feelings.'

'Thank you so much, Rod,' I said. 'That is one of the nicest things anyone has done for me.'

That last comment was a bit alcohol-fuelled, but I was being sincere. Maybe he wasn't as bad as I had first thought. So I sat and drank, and listened and listened to Rod, who kept bringing me beverages.

'I travel by myself all the time. It's really neat. I've found that I meet more people this way. Over the years, I've spoken to so many people. Like when I was in Coffs Harbour, there was this couple that I met. They were riding their bicycles from Melbourne to Brisbane.'

Beer

'Adelaide was totally neato. Their churches are really modern. I once took the tram to Glenelg and had an ice cream. It was swell. It was only when I was on the tram back, that I realised that Glenelg is spelled the same way backward as it's spelled forward. How hip! Unfortunately, none of the Adelaide locals would take a photo of me next to the sign.'

Beer

'What's with cricket? I just can't figure it out. There's a bunch of guys out in a paddock wearing white, and two of them have paddles. They whack the ball into the outfield for days and days. I just don't get it. It's not exciting like baseball, that's for sure.'

Beer

'To me, origami is absolute paradise. I can make a whole flock of cranes in just under an hour. They look a lot like the birds out on the deck there. I think they are known as 'Masked Boobies' in these parts. At least that's what Warren and the guys were saying. What do you call them in Melbourne?'

I didn't respond. I was barely listening, putting in a laugh or a grunt where I thought it might be appropriate. The preceding excitement of today's adventures had been completely dulled by Rod's alcohol and conversation. All I knew was that the guy kept getting me beers, and that was enough for me to tolerate his deep-fried ode to monotony.

'Do you call them Masked Boobies in Melbourne?' he repeated, loud enough to pierce through my shell of not-caring.

'Oh, sorry. Yeah, those birds are pretty big.'

'They kinda look like some birds that I once saw back in Florida. They just seem to know when a 'gator is in the water and don't seem flustered at all. Blah, blah, zzzz, zzzz, blah. Blah fucking blah blah blah.'

His voice had become background noise; I couldn't listen to him any longer. I started staring out through the window towards the white-ish birds on the back deck. I was right; they were pretty big. There were about seven of them, staring at us.

'Look at that lonely soul,' said the largest bird, perched on the extreme right-hand rail of the deck.

'He could be endeavouring to impress members of the opposite sex right now, but instead, he chooses to take the company of another lonely soul. Why?

Not for the pursuit of friendship, but rather for the pursuit of alcohol!' he exclaimed.

'Rark, rark, rark, rark,' the others cheered, as they flapped their wings in unison.

I could tell the talking bird was male, because he had a deep, masculine voice with a really posh accent. He sounded like a butler or the captain of the English polo team.

'I shan't begin to wonder what is to be gained from his behaviour,' he said, in between preening his feathers with his beak. 'I simply shan't.'

'Rark, rark,' the rest of them replied, with a tone of agreement in their voices.

I no longer knew how many beers I'd had, but it had to have been a lot. The drone of Rod was starting to cut in over what the huge seagull was saying. It was time to take action.

'Roderick,' I stammered, 'I think that I should go outside for a while to talk to those big boobies. They're getting cheeky. Fuck, I'm drunk.'

I looked around and got up. Without looking towards Captain American Talker, I walked outside onto the back deck. It was dark. Stumbling, I tried to take in the beauty of the moonlit water, but my alcoholic eyes wouldn't focus. I could still hear the pompous seagull's voice, but he was muttering inaudibly under his breath. I thought that he was a pretentious tool.

'How the fuck do you know what I want?' I asked, as I looked straight into the black eyes and orange beak of my accuser.

I didn't receive an answer. The seven birds took off simultaneously, making loud, flapping noises. As they disappeared into the horizon, I yelled after them.

'Don't judge me, you feathered, flapping fuckers. Fuck off back into the ocean then. You're not better than me!'

It was then I realised that I had probably yelled that a little bit too loud. But fuck, they needed to be told. At least I didn't shit wherever I happened to be sitting, or at least not very often. They were making my drinking habits sound unsociable, but I couldn't socialise sober; it was that simple. Stupid fucking seagulls, or emus, or masked boobies ...whatever they were. How can they think they are better than me? I'll show those sea-chickens.

'You all right there, guv?'

Fuck. I'd been mumbling to myself, or had I?

'Was you yelling abuse at the sea?' asked Neville, his red hair catching the moonlight. He'd sprung out of nowhere. I wondered how much he had seen and if he had also heard those pompous fowl.

'Umm, I dunno. Fuck off,' was my brilliant reply.

'Guv, them waves, do they really think they're better than you?'

'I said, FUCK OFF!'

Slumber. Dark, dreamless sleep.

I've no idea how much later it was when I woke up. I was still on the deck, flat on my back. The moon was full, lighting up the motionless sea that surrounded me. Talking birds? How crazy must I be going? I noticed a ladder. I figured I would get a better view from up the top of that ladder, so I climbed it, hoping to find those up-themselves feather-fucked pterodactyls.

I climbed slowly because I was still drunk. As I got closer to the top, I could hear strange noises.

The ladder led to a small top deck. I peered my head over the top of the ladder to see what was going on.

Warren was standing upright. In front of him was Margrit. She was bent over, her hands grabbing onto the railing. Her sarong and bikini lay next to her feet. Warren was repeatedly thrusting into her from behind. They were both being impressively quiet about it. I watched for a good fifteen minutes. When it was obvious they were about to conclude, I clambered back down the ladder towards my room.

I had a quick and quiet wank and went to sleep.

The next two days on the boat were awesome. The reef was spectacular and the beer (provided by various Asian benefactors) was cold. I think that Warren had moved on from Margrit to Heidi by the time the trip was over.

The best part was when we were presented with our Open Water Certificates. We all passed, all six of us, Neville included. We were given the option of buying a DVD of our adventures for only ninety-seven dollars. How good is that?

Pity. I had no money at all.

Still, I'd achieved something, and those birds could think whatever they wanted.

The Jendaya Chronicle: Part Two

My two brothers fell asleep. We had been driving for a long, long time. I sat in the front seat next to Mummy. I wasn't usually in the front seat: it was usually both Daddy and Mummy in the front seat. I asked Mummy where we were going and she said that we were going on a holiday to South Africa. I had never been out of Zimbabwe and was very excited. I asked Mummy if Daddy might be there, and she said he might be. I fell asleep in the front seat, feeling happy.

When I wakened, Mummy had stopped the car. It was still dark and she was talking to some policemen. All of our bags were on the side of the road. The men were in a loud discussion with her. They were talking, or yelling, in Shona, which I can speak too. We all spoke English at home.

They were saying things like, 'We need more money from you,' and 'Where are you going?'

While they did this, three or four other people had crept up from behind them. I thought they were coming to save Mummy, but all they did was steal our bags from the side of the road. Then they ran off with them. They had nearly disappeared into the darkness when the policemen noticed them. The two policemen started shooting at the group of people with our bags, until they stopped moving. The policemen then impolitely told Mummy that she should get back into the car. So, Mummy did what she was told and she started driving again. As we drove off, I could see the policemen going through the pockets of the people, who were not moving any longer.

Jabi and Emmi woke up, but remained as quiet as mice, which was unusual for them. The road got bumpier and bumpier and we all stayed silent. I didn't ask Mummy what we were doing. I didn't want to cause trouble.

Eventually, the light came back into the sky. We drove through bushes and trees. The wildebeests and zebras didn't seem to know what a car was; they didn't even run away.

The animals kept my twin brothers entertained for a while, but eventually they started getting bored. When my brothers get bored in the back of the car, they start hitting each other and crying. Mummy still didn't say anything, so I had to turn around and tell them to keep their hands to themselves. They told me that I wasn't Daddy and I couldn't tell them what to do.

I asked Mummy where Daddy was, and she still didn't say anything. She didn't cry, but I could tell that she wanted to. The bushes got thicker and thicker and we saw more and more animals. Jabi and Emmi played a game where they tried to be the first to call out an animal's name when they saw it.

They called out when they saw baboons. They called out when they saw elephants. They called out when they saw lions. They called out when they saw turkeys. They called out when they saw vultures. The animals they called out most were wildebeest and zebras. Mummy told me that we were nearly there. She didn't tell us where we were going.

We had to drive over the bushes because there were too many of them to drive around. Jabi and Emmi were quiet again. The car stopped. The sun started to go down. Mummy told us that we were going to get up very early in the morning.

I don't remember sleeping that night. When the sun started to come up Mum told us to get out of the car. We started walking. I was terribly thirsty and hungry, but we had nothing to eat or drink. We walked silently, not knowing where we were going or why. As we trudged through the bushes, Mum started singing a song that Daddy had made up. We used to sing it together when we were helping Daddy in the fields. We all sang it together, making sure we weren't too loud, for we were afraid that an animal would find us and eat us.

We plant the seed for humankind,

We plant the seed with love,

We plant the seed and pray to God,

Who looks down from above.

For if the sun and rain are kind,

And food grows far and long,

We'll feast that night and thank the Lord,

And then we'll sing this song.

The song reminded me of the farm, and of home, and it made me a little bit sad. I think we all realised at about the same time that things were never going to be the same again. So the song just sort of got quieter and quieter until we stopped all together. We kept walking until we got to a big, wire fence. It seemed to go forever and ever in both directions. There was barbed wire on the top of it. Mum told us that we had to get to the other side of the fence and out of Zimbabwe forever.

Missives Of Merpeople

Dear Father,

I hope the corals have passed my message to you promptly. I'm sorry I haven't been able to communicate sooner. My journey has had many challenges and has affected my ability to remember my mission, let alone keep in touch with you, my sire.

In an effort to blend in with the land population, I have had to pretend that I am obsessed with money, which I then must spend on a mild poison known as alcohol. Alcohol is a liquid substance that seems to have the same effect as Krasskalweed. They drink it for pleasure, until it makes them sick.

I know that you abhor the idea of money and wealth, but it seems increasingly important for the land population. To get money, one needs to have a job. By working in a job, one gives time and services to a master. He or she rewards one with money, which can then be spent on poisonous alcohol.

The alcohol can be quite discombobulating, and after one pot of 'Carlton Draught' I seem to become a little bit 'pissed', as they call it here. During the next sunrise, my memory and sensory systems are even more weakened than they already are due to my mission, causing me the need to spend some time in the ocean almost immediately. These days, I can resemble a land-dweller while in the water unless I wish to change forms.

I have become quite fond of some of their pop music, and quite often listen to the modern stylings of Robert Palmer on my personal stereo.

Without alcohol or any of the other drugs that the aggregation known as 'Cairns' relies on, I am able to stay comfortably out of the water for two to three days. It also helps if I eat salt whilst in the shower, a shower being a reverse of our bubble-cleansers.

My mission is to report back as much information as possible to the Sect of Ever-loving Enlightenment, so infiltration into the ground-settlement is an absolute must.

I will send word as soon as I have clearance to return. Please do not disclose any of this information to anybody, lest we raise concerns.

Yours in Honour,

Your first-spawned son.

Dear Son,

We understand that your mission is important to yourself and your flowery group of no-hopers, but we still advise that you return home immediately. We are concerned about this alcohol dependency of the dry land. If alcohol is anything like Krasskalweed, then you should stay well away. Incidentally, your mother wants to know where you have tried Krasskalweed before. Please don't tell her I gave you some on your sixteenth birthday.

Preparations for the Mollusc Festival are upon us and the community could have done with your help. Your sisters miss you as well. We want you to come home, and not home to that group of no-hoping misfits who sent you away in the first instance. True Merpeople are loyal to their family.

I feel compelled to tell you the story of The Man and the Dolphin. You listened to it from the time of your spawning. Maybe it is time you listened again.

A long, long time ago, a young boy and a young dolphin were best friends. They met each other at the beach and played in the shallows all day. They told each other about their homes and their families.

'Our family sits around a table and has lamb for dinner,' the boy said.

'Our family hunts fish and squid for dinner,' the dolphin said.

'We have to be careful that we don't get attacked by the people in our neighbouring village,' the boy said.

'We have to be careful that we don't get attacked by sharks,' the dolphin said.

During the day these two were inseparable. Every evening the boy returned to his village, and the dolphin returned to the ocean to swim with his pod.

One morning, the boy said, 'I cannot come here to play tomorrow. Tomorrow I have to build bridges with my father.'

'I understand,' said the dolphin. 'I will miss you very much.'

The boy embraced the dolphin and then watched him swim out to sea for the last time.

The boy worked hard with his father. Day after day he built bridges. He missed his best friend but worked so hard he did not have time to think about it. Ultimately, the boy forgot about his friend the dolphin.

The boy slowly became bigger and stronger. Eventually, he became a man.

The man met a beautiful woman and married her. He built a house and had three children. He wanted to make more money to care for his family so he decided to build a fishing boat. His fishing boat was the biggest in his village.

The day came when he sailed the boat out to sea. The man cast huge nets into the water. His net filled with sharks, turtles, mermaids, stingrays, eels, sea serpents, whales, seals, crocodiles, dolphins, dugongs, fish and all that was beautiful in the ocean.

'This is a great living,' thought the man. 'I will be a millionaire soon.'

He returned home to his family that night with fish and money.

'Tomorrow, I will come home with twice as many fish and make twice as much money,' he told his wife.

The man did exactly that. He returned home each day with more and more money for his family. Eventually, he made enough money to buy a fleet of boats. He sent armies of men out to take what they could from the ocean.

Once, while fishing, the man dragged his full net into the boat. He noticed a dolphin was stuck in his nets. He recognised the dolphin from his childhood.

'Why do you do this? You do not need to send out a whole fleet of boats every day. You have enough already. Why must you take more from my ocean than you need?' asked the dolphin.

'I do this for the progress of mankind. We build cities and weapons. We make beautiful works of art. We

*can create fire. We are much smarter than dolphins,'
said the man.*

*'We do not hurt one another. We do not start wars
with other pods of dolphins. We do not pollute the
world and change its shape to suit ourselves. We love
our world and keep it beautiful,' said the dolphin, as
he perished in the bright sunshine.*

*The man emptied his net into the boat, and cast it
back into the ocean.*

*Son, the Merpeople live an existence harmonious with
the sea, like our dolphin friends. I know you will make
the right decision.*

Honour always,

Your Father.

Chapter Seven

As much as I loved being on the boat, it was great to be back on land and to be able to get away from Rod. Steve was not glad to see me back at his Hostel, but he knew he had to let me stay there for five more days. I took the opportunity to remind him that his comb-over looked awesome.

Life went back to normal, mopping floors badly, collecting the dole, living in the hostel, pretending to have friends, stealing morsels of food and alcohol and trying to get laid.

After a couple of days, it seemed like I'd never got my Open Water Certificate at all. Nobody at the hostel seemed impressed: they had either 'been there, done that', or they didn't understand the beauty of it at all. I soon forgot what the initial purpose of the exercise had been.

Oh, yeah! Fuck. That sea cucumber diving job with that fat prick. We were supposed to start soon, but I didn't know when. Arriving at Beche De Mer Diving, I was greeted by the same yappy dog which, again, eventually ran away. Victoria answered the door, looking as cool as ever.

'What time do we start? Is it tomorrow?' I spat at her nervously.

'Meet us at Trinity Wharf at six in the morning.'

'Okay. Where?'

'Just look for Jesse and me.'

'Are you on the boat with us?'

'Yeah, I'm the cook and a very good diver too.'

Awesome.

The next morning, I was riding high in the sky on the back of a giant red dragon. His name was Roderick; but unlike my relationship with his American namesake, we were best friends. He would do anything I asked.

'Let us burn Innisfail and all the bogans that dwell within, dear Rod,' I said.

'Roooaarrr,' said Rod in agreement.

As we descended from above the clouds and onto the small town, panicked people ran for cover. We flew close enough to hear their individual screams.

'Cause mayhem and bloodshed my crimson companion. Posthaste!' I commanded.

As quick as lightning, Rod picked up a school bus in one of his massive claws. He let it drop over the local church. I shall never know what happened next, because something in my subconscious jolted me back into the real world.

Shit! We were late! Fucking Neville; he told me that he'd set his alarm. I shook the useless fucker awake. I think I also woke a French guy in our room.

'Come on, Ginger!' I yelled. 'That skipper guy will go nuts. We'll miss the boat.'

'Orright, steady on, convict,' he retorted, still asleep.

'Hey!' I yelled. 'I'm looking forward to being out at sea with just you, me and other Aussies—try and pull that shit when the only laws are mob rule.'

'Your thieving great-great-grandparents obviously didn't enforce mob rule when they were deported over 'ere, did they now? If they 'ad, they would 'ave mutinied, returned to Ol' Blighty, and you'd 'ave been British.'

'A curse I wouldn't wish on anyone, except fucking poms like you.'

'Stop this bickering and let me rest my French head, you gay lovers!'

And then we left. We caught a taxi to Trinity Wharf and got there at 6:32 a.m. Not too bad, I thought. We still had no idea what boat we were looking for, but that also gave us a good excuse for being late.

Yes, we were late, but it was still early and hot. Fuck. I needed a beer.

We ran, searching throughout the different fingers of the marina, not really knowing what we were looking for. I was beginning to think that the boat had left without us when I saw the unmistakeable silhouette of Jesse Barnes. He stood at the end of Jetty Three, looking fat and angry. I nearly went back to the hostel then and there, but the man had seen me—it was too late. We walked hurriedly towards him.

'G'day, boys. How's it going?' he asked.

Surprised by his reaction, I said, 'Good, mate. Yeah, good. Sorry we're late.'

'Don't matter much. Probably won't get out until about eleven.'

'Oh, good,' I said.

'Yeah, you can head off and come back around nine. No worries.'

'Yeah, thanks for letting us know, guv,' said Neville, sarcastically.

We walked back to the hostel. It took about an hour. We decided to go along the boardwalk that runs alongside the filthy mudflats known as Cairns Beach. Beach? Yeah, right! The only things that sunned themselves on that shitty cesspit were crabs, mudskippers and super-deadly cone-shells. On our return we had a couple of joints, a couple of fridge-donated beers, and went back to sleep.

I was a face-washer floating around in a bathtub. I was weightless and warm. The soapy water ran throughout my being. If I concentrated, I could control my direction. I weaved in and around the legs and arms of the lady that was taking a bath. I was picked out of the water and rubbed against a pair of breasts. I was starting to think that this was not such a bad existence, when something in the back of my mind jolted me into the conscious world.

Shit! We were late again! Neville told me he'd set the alarm again, the still-useless fucker. I pummelled him with my pillow to wake him up. He didn't seem to quite get the message, so I yelled at him,using an American military voice:

'OFFICER NEVILLE! YOU GODDAM USELESS SACK OF CRAP! ON THE FLOOR AND GIVE ME TWENTY NOW. I SAID NNNOOWWW!'

'YOU ARE A WOMBAT SHAGGING CUNT!'

'SACRE BLEU! FUQUE OFF LE FAGGOTS!'

And we were off.

That time, at least, we knew where we were supposed to be going, even if we were late again.

As we approached the boat, there were more people hanging around. Getting closer I recognised Victoria. She was wearing the same brown cords and looking good. I also recognised Stan from the hostel, and that little dog. It was running around yapping at people. Jesse Barnes was there. He was standing on the jetty, using large hand gestures to explain something to two other guys. I didn't know who they were.

Barnes saw us and signalled gruffly for us to come over to him.

'Boys,' he said, 'these are two of the other guys working on the boat for this trip.'

He paused.

'Well, introduce yourselves to each other. I'm not the bloody hostess of this party,' he said, laughing as he walked towards the boat.

It was obvious the captain had no idea what any of our names were.

'Nathan,' said the shorter of the two guys as he extended his hand.

'Neville.'

'Kelvin.'

'Paul Hart,' said the tall guy.

'Neville.'

'Kelvin.'

And that was as far as our conversation got. The four of us stared out towards the water, none of us trying to break the silence. We were about to spend three weeks together, in close proximity, with nowhere to run.

Chapter Eight

He may not have known all our names, but Captain Jesse Barnes took to ordering us around quite quickly.

'Hey, old mate!' he said. 'Put the fish bins on the top deck.'

I had no idea if I was even going to get paid for this. I had no idea why I was doing it. Still, I jumped at his every request.

'I SAID THE FISH BINS, NOT THE FUCKING MUSSEL BINS!'

Again, I pondered the why-the-fucks of what I was doing.

The boat hadn't left the marina. It was a pretty big fucker of a boat. It looked 20 metres long and 5 metres wide, all ocean-blue. It had these big, skeletal, metal wings that were tied up in the air, so they couldn't flap. I had seen other boats like it when I was waiting to go out with Specialised Divers but I hadn't thought about what they did.

Neville stacked bags of salt up against a wall. I stacked mussel—no, sorry—fish bins, on the top deck. The other guys relayed food from the back of the ute; Victoria grabbed boxes, one at a time, from out of the tray and passed them to Paul, who walked a few steps along the pier and passed them to

Nathan, who stood on the boat. Nathan then passed them down a hatch in the middle of the front deck. Stan stood down in the hatch, freezing his largish pecs off. It was his job to stack twenty one days' worth of food in the massive freezer, at the same time dealing with weather conditions the absolute opposite to the rest of Cairns.

Victoria disappeared with the ute, taking that stupid, yapping, sex-aid of a dog.

It was close to eleven in the morning and I was already tired. I hadn't worked like that before; I was usually still asleep. Barnes, who didn't give a shit, called us all in.

'Right,' he said. 'As soon as our chef gets back, we're gonna get cracking. If you wanna be a slack prick and take a break, take it now.'

I thought that to be a great idea. I climbed up a ladder that led to the top deck, which was smaller and full of barrels, ropes and other crap that had been tied down. All of the gear looked old and sea worn, like Barnes himself. I sat down in a soft looking pile of ropes, and tried to force myself into slumbersville, hoping that maybe I'd get transformed back into a face-washer. I had just dozed off when I was woken up by a loud, rumbling sound.

The engines were on and the boat was moving. I sprang to my feet and looked down onto the bottom deck. They were untying ropes and pulling tyres up from the outside of the boat—even Neville was helping. They seemed to have it sorted, so I lay back down. The rumbling of the engine made the floor of the upper deck vibrate. It rocked me back to sleep.

When I woke up, I could see water all around me. I had no idea which direction we were going or where we were. I didn't care: all I wanted to do was vomit. I hurried down the ladder and hurled my guts out. Luckily for everybody else, I was able to project it all off the back of the boat and out into the sea. I was hunched over the back railing for what seemed like seventeen fucking years.

Occasionally, I sensed someone walking past me, but I didn't look up. I don't think anyone cared too much about my state of being.

After forcing half of my body weight out of my mouth, I found my way down the front deck and into our cabin. I crawled into my bunk bed and tried desperately to sleep. There were no sweet dreams that time. There was only the enduring nausea and pain of seasickness.

I was the sleeping-awake; the living-dead; an immobilized zombie. I could not slumber, yet neither could I move, talk, or do anything else. I was starting to think that I had actually transformed into the mattress that I was lying on, so lacking was I in signs of life. Hours went by and I lay semi-conscious on the bunk bed. I could hear the engine really well down there. It was very, very loud. It was so loud in fact, that only the crustiest old sea dog would have been able to get some shut-eye.

The cabin hatch was closed completely, eliminating any light. It was completely dark inside my private little hell. I opened my eyes occasionally, only to see the same things I saw with my eyes shut. There was just darkness and, eventually, thankfully, sleep.

'Oy, Mexican! What's going on 'ere, then?' asked Neville.

It took me a while to work out where I was before I could answer Neville's stupidly obvious question.

'I am running a marathon in order to raise awareness of the fact that there are bony pommies around, like you, who have still not been sterilised or shot. I paused. 'What the fuck does it look like? I'm fucking seasick as a dog.'

'All right Mexican, settle down. I'm just down 'ere to tell you dinner's on, innit? And the skip, 'oo's not 'appy with you at the moment, says that you're on watch between one and three this morning. All right then, Mexican?'

Neville must have learned the new name from the other guys on the boat. Queenslanders called anyone from south of Queensland 'Mexicans'— especially Victorians. It shitted me up the wall, although I couldn't show that to Neville for a second, lest I be blessed as 'Mexican' for the rest of the trip— which I most likely had been anyway.

I doubted most Queenslanders would have even known that Mexico was south of the border of the USA. Most of them wouldn't have known there was a world beyond their bucket-bong.

'Neville,' I said, trying to be as nice and not-pissed-off as I could, 'I don't think I'll be coming up for dinner, and I have no fucking idea what to do on watch. Should I come up and talk to Jesse?'

'Nah, you can leave that out, guv,' he said. 'He said that Stan will wake you up and show you the ropes. So should I tell the skip its back to beddy-bye for the poor, invalid-Mexican-Indian-subserviant-no-ticker-no-stomach-emu-shagger?'

'That would be appreciated,' I replied. I shut my eyes and listened to Neville climbing up the ladder. He farted every second rung he climbed, giggling like a schoolgirl. The door clanged shut and complete darkness replaced the reddish-black in my eyelids. I stared at with my eyes closed for hours, until I heard the guys coming back in. I pretended to be asleep.

'She was up for it all the time. No matter where we were or what we were doing, that dirty whore wanted to cop it. Of course, I think it had to do with me being an awesome root.' I thought that it was Nathan talking.

'Once I was at Shenanigans and I worked out that I had rooted half of the chicks that were there. Seriously! The other half I wouldn't go near, anyway.'

It went on for a while:

'…I get pulled over by a female copper and end up getting a blow job on the side of the road. As soon as she saw me she was wet…'

'…rooting this chick, right, when her husband comes in. He swings at me, so I jump out of his wife and deck him while I'm still naked. So he's lying on the floor, unconscious, and I go back to his missus and start banging her again…'

'…rooting away when the security guard comes over…getting pretty aggro…knocked him out cold…ended up fucking his missus…'

'…didn't like my attitude…his girlfriend and his sister at the same time…fourteen shots of bourbon…decked the cunt…'

Neville threw in an odd comment every now and then, but Nathan was driving the conversation. Paul stayed silent, and I think Stan was absent. I prayed for sleep, or death, to take me.

Eventually Nathan stopped. Only the sound of the engine could be heard—at least initially. And then, above the roar of the massive motor, I heard a faint, pounding beat.

Ump ump

Ump ump

Ump ump

And then it stopped.

Then it started again, but with a different tempo.

Ump ump ump

Ump ump ump

What the fuck?

The possibilities of what that noise could be ran through my head. Did Neville have a dodgy pacemaker somehow jammed into that tiny chest? Was somebody attempting to have a quiet wank? Was it the mating call of the cabin frogs? It was too loud for frogs, maybe cabin elephants? Lastly, there was one thing I kept coming back to.

Was I going completely out of my fucking mind?

Ump ump

Ump ump

Ump ump ump

Ump ump

Perhaps I was.

I listened to the real (or imagined) deep and pulsating beat.

Ump ump

Ump ump

Ump ump

I stayed in that state for hours, until the door opened.

'Oy, old mate, time for youse to garn watch, ay?' said Stan Dwyer.

Guessing that he was referring to me, I jumped off the top bunk and made my way up the ladder, making sure I farted before closing the door.

Dwyer lead me up to the wheelhouse. I felt sick.

'So, youse basically just sit here, mate. Youse watch the radar and the computer screen. If youse see anything within five nautical miles of the boat, youse wake up Barnes, ay?' he explained.

'Youse also got to plot our course on the map every twenty minutes, ay? By doing that youse...'

Getting sicker and sicker. Not listening to Stan at all. Trying as hard as possible not to...

Hmmphh...hhmpph...Bllooorrr!

Because I was indoors, I had to initially hold the vomit in my mouth. I could taste the cheesy goodness down my throat as I ran out of the wheelhouse and towards the back deck. I chose my usual throwing-up spot. We humans are such creatures of habit. After ten minutes of heaving, I wiped my face, nostrils and bloodshot eyes and wobbled back to the wheelhouse. When I got there Stan was gone.

So I sat and watched the black ocean, vomiting every twenty minutes. When a wave of nausea came over me, I knew it was time to plot our course on the map. I didn't know how to do this so I put crosses on the map in roughly the same pattern as the other previous crosses. Where we were, I really didn't know. I saw no boats, lights, or anything during the whole two hours I was there. Staring and vomiting. Vomiting and staring. It was a glamorous existence. Finally it got to three a.m., which meant I could go back to sleep after waking up Neville—which I did with pleasure.

I started off by slapping his cheeks gently. Gradually the slaps got harder and harder, until the pain woke him up.

'What the fuck?' he exclaimed.

'Little ginger man, you're on watch. NOW! Get to it.'

'You sick bastard. That's out of order, innit?'

'Actually, I'm not that sick anymore, I'm feeling quite a lot better. Thanks for asking.'

He jumped out of his bunk and climbed up the stairs. As he slammed the door shut I could hear him muttering something about 'fucking Mexicans.'

Feeling satisfied and tired, I climbed back into my bunk.

Ump ump

Ump ump

Ump ump

The beat put me back to sleep, pulsing in unison with my heart and soul.

Chapter Nine

After living on the boat for eight days, the seasickness dissipated. It seemed like Cairns and Melbourne had never existed. I couldn't picture having lived anywhere else. The open ocean was my life. Blue water was all that could be seen in any direction. Sometimes it was a riot of waves, sometimes a carpet of serenity.

Our sleeping quarters were cramped, to say the least. Once you managed to open the hatch and climb down the ladder, there was a walking area the size of a board-game. It was usually covered with clothes, bags and pornography. The triangular room had four bunk beds on the two side walls. They were so tiny that I had to contort myself into an 'S' bend to fit my whole frame onto the thin mattress.

I slept in the top bunk, on the left as you came in. Neville's bunk was beneath mine. The other wall was for Nathan and Paul Hart. I think Paul was on the bottom. During the night, our dingy quarters smelled of sea cucumber, body odour and farts. Stan got to sleep somewhere else, because he had the honour of being ordered around like a bitch all day by Jesse Barnes.

Despite the decor, I looked forward to getting into the cabin and sleeping. Each day's labour was always harder than the last. My body certainly wasn't used to it at all and I invariably passed out within minutes of collapse.

A typical day went something like this one:

At 4:45 a.m., the door of the cabin opened. A stream of unwelcome sunlight cut through the dankness.

'Wakey, wakey, hands off snakey!' Barnes bellowed into our cell before clanging the door shut.

'I'm going to murder that cunt.' My usual first thought for the day.

It was up to us to start moving ourselves—a slow process. Neville's bunk was the closest to the light switch and he had a habit of ignoring the wake-up call and going back to sleep. We threw magazines and CDs in his direction to get him to turn on the light.

Once illumination was achieved, we marched zombie-like up the ladder towards the back deck and stood, the four of us in a row, and pissed over the side of the boat.

We stared out into the ocean for about ten minutes, until Stan the Man came up from the lower galley and told us in his own special way that it was time for breakfast.

The lower galley was completely off-limits for the four cabin boys, except during dinner and breakfast. Barnes always made it known to us that we were privileged to be down there. He'd make remarks about how shitty our sleeping quarters were, or tell us off for not looking happy. Victoria, Barnes, and Stan all had their own rooms down there, somewhere.

I couldn't tell you whose room was whose: we were never permitted to stay down there and have a look around. I really wanted to suss out if they had any alcohol.

Victoria made breakfast. It was nutritious and pretty plain. Barnes didn't want us getting hot breakfasts. He didn't want us using up time before we got to work. So we—that is, everybody except the captain— didn't get hot breakfasts. Barnes, on the other hand, did. Barnes had Victoria prepare muffins and eggs for him. We ate bread and Vegemite. Barnes drank orange juice. We drank cordial. Barnes had yoghurt on his muesli. We had Home Brand long-life skim milk on our Weetbix. Barnes drank Moccona coffee. We made do with some brown, powdery shit made by a company that most likely stopped producing in the late '70s. Barnes was not one of the boys. It was his boat, his rules, and he didn't want to be mistaken for one of us, not even at the breakfast table.

After breakfast, we changed into our stained cucumber clothes and repacked the previous day's catch.

The sea cucumbers didn't appreciate being gutted and stuffed with salt while they were still alive. They protested against it by leeching out litres of slimy gunk overnight. By morning, the sealed barrels were bursting with sea cucumber juice. We took each individual corpse out of the barrels, wiped it off, stuffed it with more salt, and put it into another sealed container. By the end of it, there was thick cucumber juice everywhere. It sucked balls and it was still really early in the morning.

Stan Dwyer owned a big, loud CD player. His collection of music was a small one. We listened to Green Day's Dookie during re-pack. Sometimes we'd listen to Rage Against The Machine's Evil Empire or Marilyn Manson's Antichrist Superstar. I don't think Dwyer had heard of music post-1995.

Once we'd repacked the salty slugs and put them back into a room much bigger than our cabin, it was time to start diving and to hopefully make some money.

You only got paid for what you caught. If you caught nothing, you got paid nothing. It went directly against my general attitude towards work and broke two of my golden rules:

1. Do not do more than you need to at any time.

2. Rule one particularly applies when you are not under direct supervision from your boss or supervisor.

Unfortunately, if I'd stuck to my rules, the only person I'd have been ripping off would have been myself. So when I was diving, it was game-fucking-on.

Drifting under the water was a lot of fun. If we hadn't had to hunt defenceless echinoderms, it would have been the most awesome job ever. But we did, and it was hard work.

The creature itself is not a stealthy beast of the water. It moves at the rate of thirty centimetres a decade. It eats sand and shits out slightly cleaner sand. There are different types of sea cucumber, and they are worth different amounts of money. The main type we were after was the White Teat, because it was worth the most money. It looked like, and acted like, a cowpat. Once spotted, they were easy to pick up. Spotting them, and then getting to them before you had drifted past, was the hard part.

I was usually diving at the same time as Victoria and Neville. There was no honour system between the three of us. If they saw a White Teat first, even if it was in my area, they'd grab it. Neville was particularly fond of cutting my grass. He'd give me the big 'V' salute as he swam back to his zone, where he fucking should have been the whole time.

The landscapes we went over were fucking awesome. There were fan-like corals, tree-like corals, and corals that looked like huge brains. The chains crashed through whatever was in front of them. They were the huge, clunky hunks of metal which drove massive highways through Coral Town on every dive. We hung onto a rope that was attached to the heavy chains, providing us with transport. We also breathed from a regulator, attached to a fucking long yellow hose, providing us with air. The hose went all the way back to the mothership. We were not permitted to let go of the rope, or stop breathing from the regulator. Barnes would have gone ballistic if one of us died.

Wherever we went, we were followed by snakes. They never seemed angry or aggressive, just curious, which still freaked me out —they were venomous snakes. I wouldn't hang out with an armed, psychopathic killer just because he didn't have a murderous look about him. Still, there wasn't much you could do about them. Like with Neville, you just had to pretend that they weren't there and hope they didn't bite you.

And I had a good distraction from the wildlife: the almighty pursuit of sea cucumbers. Grabbing the rope with one hand and supporting a huge net-bag hybrid with my neck, I scooted along the bottom, binning anything that looked remotely like a sea cucumber with my spare hand. Sometimes they'd be in plain view, lying on the sand. Often they were hiding among the rocks and coral. Every now and then I would miss a lucky one while busy pursuing others. I was down there for twenty-five minutes at a time, and if I had been circled by great white sharks, it wouldn't have taken my attention off the task at hand. The cucumbers were the priority.

I was naturally pretty good at this diving gig. I could control my buoyancy and direction easily and I was developing an eye for the cucumbers. I was stealing more slugs from Neville and Nathan than they were from me. It was a good feeling.

As good as I was getting, I was still not in the same league as Victoria. She consistently came up with more than any of the other boys. Except for Paul, that is. If I was in a different league than Victoria, then Paul Hart was in a different league, being played on a different planet. The guy was unbelievable. He must have sung a high-frequency siren call that was irresistible to the cucumbers. On hearing it, they would grow fins and swim directly for his neck-bag, fighting for the privilege to enter his swag of death.

The few times I was in the water with him, I studied his behaviour as best I could. He was pretty tall, and his fin kicks gave him a lot of power. Sometimes I looked to my right and couldn't see him anywhere. He had left the chains and his rope and had gone off on his own. Ten minutes later, he'd be back, neck-bag full of White Teat.

I asked him about it when we were back on deck.

'What's your secret? How do you catch so many, mate?'

In reply, he shrugged his shoulders and walked off. That was a boundary between us broken. By shrugging in my direction, he had acknowledged my existence.

I felt like I belonged under the water. Barnes could not yell at me when I was in the ocean. Neville couldn't shit me up the cabin walls, and Nathan couldn't bore me with stories about rooting chicks up the arse. There was also loads of cool stuff down there.

Once, a school of Giant Trevally charged around me during my oxygen hang. One moment there was nothing, and then for two seconds, a herd of silver beasts was all around me. Then they were gone. Awesome.

Our oxygen hang was at the end part of the dive. We hung on to a rope and breathed pure oxygen, from a special separate hose and mouthpiece, until our Captain banged on the side of the Beche De Mer. Barnes wouldn't tell me why we had to hang like shark-bait and breath medical tasting gas, but Victoria was happy to explain it to me. If we didn't flush the nitrogen out of our bloodstream with oxygen we would almost certainly die of the bends. The hangs got longer and longer the more diving we did, which was especially fine if I was sharing the line with Victoria.

Occasionally, I would forget about collecting sea cucumbers. I'd fly through the water, pretending to be a superhero, drifting away from the reality of life. For the first time ever, I had found a place where I belonged.

I'd even figured out what that rhythm was; the pulsing, beating sound that resounded through my nights. At first, all I could hear was the repetitive Ump in different time signatures and speeds. It dominated my hours of darkness. But, when I listened hard enough, I could make out some melodies that sounded familiar. Slowly, they became more and more recognizable.

 One night, when I was resisting the urge to jack-off to thoughts of Victoria, it hit me. It was 'Simply Irresistible!' by Robert Palmer, followed by 'Addicted to Love,' and then the yodelling one by Robert Palmer, then 'The Heat is On' and so on. Every night I would hear subliminal Robert Palmer tracks. I didn't know if it was the ocean causing the music, if Robert himself was singing from the grave, or if it was one of my voices.

All theories were squashed when I saw Paul Hart taking off his headphones one morning. Shortly after, he ejected a CD from his walkman, gave the shiny side a quick polish, and returned it into the player.

That was what I had been listening to: Paul's Best of Robert Palmer album. The mystery had gone and I was a little disappointed. Still, Robert Palmer helped both Paul and me to get to sleep, forming a bond between me and the man that let his sea cucumber tally do the talking.

Missives Of Merpeople

Dear Father,

I am sorry, but I simply do not have the clearance to return yet. I shall return only when my brethren want me to. They are aware of our communication, using the coral network, and are sympathetic to my needs to regularly converse with you. However, returning is not possible until I find out more about the earth-dwellers. Aside from that, I don't want to leave, especially now that the Saints are in the finals.

There is much for me to see here, and much for me to learn. I can almost hold a short conversation with another land-dweller.

Maybe I should not have started my journey at the fast-paced society of Cairns. It can be as busy as the reefs off its shores. I think surely other cities must be smaller and less frantic.

My next big challenge is to gain a 'sense of humour.' Humour is a term I am not familiar with and cannot understand at all. All I know is that many humans ask me where my sense of humour is, or if I have one. It seems to be the key to gaining information from people.

I am finding it easier to ingest alcohol, and have tried a hot inhalant known as 'marijuana.' It is harsh on my gills and I cannot tolerate it at the moment. Other people seem to find me 'humorous' if they have been inhaling the smoke from these marijuana cigarettes.

It may make you happy to know that I have acquired a job that allows me to regularly quench my skin with life-giving sea water. It has been my duty to take sea cucumbers out of the ocean and prepare them to be consumed by the land dwellers. My job is on a boat.

I have been pretending to use a breathing device that is unnecessary to me. I have also had to be much less proficient than my abilities allow. Still, my ego ensures that I catch and kill more sea cucumbers than any land dweller in my company.

Your loyal son.

Dear Son,

Honour has forced me to contact the authorities regarding your job. I went straight to the Head Squihhsbah. He, like me, takes a very dim view of boats and their inhabitants. However, all he can do is ask you to return, as I do.

I feel ashamed that I raised you to join a band of dangerous hippies. I feel even worse that they then sent you to the forbidden dry land on a bizarre, open-

ended fact-finding mission. I fear they have taken control of your thoughts and emotions and are using them for their own ends.

I must have told you the wrong stories when you were growing up. I should have told you the one about the flying fish that took one look at the land dwellers, realised how treacherous they were, and disappeared back into the ocean, never to return. Or the one about the penguins that fall over when arching their head back to look at the humans' flying machines overhead—although I must admit I do not know the moral to that story. However, the moral of this tale is obvious:

'The squid was living a happy life. All day she swam in the great oceans with her family. The family was made up of thousands of other squid just like her; they all had two large eyes and ten long tentacles. She loved swimming with her family.

Her father was the wisest squid of all. He taught her about all of the creatures in the ocean. She asked him about lobsters.

'The lobster is shy and hides behind the rocks,' her father said.

'When the moon and the sun both shine bright, the lobster will crawl for miles and miles along the ocean floor. That is when we shall hunt them.'

She asked him about turtles.

'The turtle looks slow and gentle, but do not be fooled,' he said.

'It is afraid of nothing in the ocean. We must be wary of the turtle at all times, otherwise it will eat us.'

She asked him about seaweed.

'Seaweed is a mysterious life-form. It grows and watches life from the one spot. The seaweed talks among itself,' he said. 'It knows everything that has ever happened in the sea.'

The squid grew bigger and bigger and became smarter and smarter. She knew of sharks and whales, serpents and mermaids. She thought she knew everything there was to know about the ocean.

One day, the squid and her family were playing in the shallows. She saw in the distance some of her family struggling to swim, before they disappeared through the surface of the water. She could not see what was dragging her family out of the ocean.

'What is happening?' she asked her father.

'I did not tell you about this before,' her father said. 'That is a net; it captures everything in the ocean and takes it away. You must swim away now.'

The squid did as she was told. As she was swimming away she saw the rest of her family, including her father, being dragged out of the ocean by the net. The net was also filled with sharks, turtles, mermaids, stingrays, eels, sea serpents, whales, seals, crocodiles, dolphins, dugongs, fish and anything that was beautiful in the ocean.

The squid was alone. She missed her family, especially her father. She was so sad she swam alone into the depths of the ocean; deeper and deeper. The ocean became darker and darker. The sun's light could not reach her in the deepest parts of the ocean.

It was so dark that the squid could not see, so her eyes began to grow bigger and bigger. Very soon the squid could see perfectly.

She missed her family very much. She was sad and angry. Every night, when the sun hid away, she swam out from the depths. With her big eyes she could see lobsters and fish to hunt. She wrapped her ten tentacles around them before they even saw her coming.

Every night the squid hunted. She became bigger and bigger. She stopped hunting crabs and lobsters and started hunting sharks and turtles.

*The Giant Squid still lives in the depths of the ocean.
She will only ever come out at night to hunt her food,
and she stays as far away from nets as she can.'*

*Your loyalty should be to me. Your loyalty should not
to be to the sect, not to the earth-dwellers and not to
your job. You have spent too much time astray, and
you must return to face the consequences. It is a
matter of honour. I expect to see you soon.*

Honour always,

Your Father.

Chapter Ten

Before each dive we strapped a dive computer, handed to us by Barnes, around our wrists. These things looked like a watch combined with a laptop. They were big. I had seen all the staff at Specialised Divers wearing similarly bulbous monstrosities.

'Probably to compensate for sumthin', innit?' was Neville's observation at the time.

'So, what is that woman instructor over there compensating for by wearing a dive watch?'

'Well, she's got small knockers, 'ain't she?'

I knew that Warren certainly didn't need compensation for anything.

Barnes insisted that we have one of these on at all times when we were diving. Mine was marked number six.

'It tells me how deep you've gone down, and if you've fucked up and gone too deep. Just fucking wear the fucking thing, and if you lose it, I'll kill you. Don't go below thirty-five metres, because the watch will tell me,' was his friendly advice to us.

When we went into the water, the watches started beeping. They beeped as the chains dropped down into the depths, dragging us, via our rope, down with them. If we went upward, they beeped. Sometimes, my watch beeped at me when nothing had happened for a while—probably out of boredom. It beeped most often when I was climbing up the rope to deposit the contents of my neck-bag into the bigger net-bin, before going back for more of that sweet old 'beche de mer'—which is an industry term, I found out, for sea cucumbers. In between beeping, the watch flashed up all kinds of different numbers. Sometimes, there were three different sets of numbers on the screen at one time. I didn't know what they meant. I saw Stan sometimes consulting his watch between sea cucumbers, but the other divers never seemed to care.

Barnes treated those dive computers like they were his children; children that he liked and was fond of. I sincerely hoped he didn't have any children. The thought of him getting a shag was beyond wrong.

As soon as we got back on deck, he'd squawk two questions at us, flapping his arms in the air:

'How much fucking slug did you catch?' and, 'Did you lose that computer? Because if you fucking did....'

The shaking of one's head, while displaying your wrist with dive computer intact, was usually enough to stop him from carrying on with his threat. Seeing the object of his un-hatred, he'd take it off your wrist. I don't know where he put them when they weren't in use—probably he slept with them; they were the closest things he had to friends.

Fortunately for me, my response to the first question was usually a good one.

'Forty-odd White Teat, maybe a bit of misso,' usually kept him only angry, as distinct from livid. 'Misso' was a blanket term for any catchable sea cucumber that wasn't a White Teat. I think it was short for 'miscellaneous.' There was no room on the boat for big words like miscellaneous.

He usually saved his livid face for Neville, who was marginally behind Nathan and Stan in the slug tally.

'Fucking thirty-three slugs! What the fuck are you doing down there? Singing "God save the fucking Queen?"'

Neville usually loved verbal confrontation, but with Barnes it was different. Jesse Barnes yelled with a threatening stance, a reddening face and a voice that went up by the octave the madder he got. He didn't listen to what others said. If you replied to him, he just yelled louder and higher, flapping his arms, and eventually crescendoed with something like:

'THIS IS MY BOAT, AND IF YOU DON'T FUCKING LIKE IT, YOU'RE MORE THAN WELCOME TO JUMP OVERBOARD RIGHT NOW, YOU STUPID FUCKING CUNT!'

Neville did his best to ignore the big man, acknowledging him only if he had to. As a byproduct of all that continuous pummelling, Neville turned quiet and introspective—similar to Paul Hart while being not nearly as good a diver. His meekness extended to his whole persona. At the dinner table, he was meek. In the cabin, he was mild. If he was smoking on the top deck, he was meagre. It was as if Barnes was around him 24/7, with a threatening glare.

I liked this scared, scarred Neville. He was quiet and even courteous sometimes. He bumped into me once and said, 'Sorry, guv.' True story, that.

But Neville, despite his genetic Pomminess, didn't deserve that kind of treatment. He wasn't a bad diver—he wasn't as shit-hot as me— but he wasn't bad. We were all making money and, therefore, Barnes was probably making more money. I don't know what the cranky bastard wanted from us. He must have expected nobody to be at the bottom of the list.

In my head, I calculated (very roughly) that, if things kept going the way they were, I was going to earn two grand by the end of the mission. I couldn't spend any money on booze and drugs out at sea, which was great for saving cash. If it hadn't been for the angry-walrus captain, the 4:45 a.m. starts, the toxic guts of the sea cucumbers and the fuckheads I had to live and work with, it would have been the perfect job.

OK, let me rephrase that. Being out on a boat with Victoria and Victoria alone would have been the perfect job. She seemed to handle every challenge with ease: diving, appeasing the captain, and feeding the lot of us. She was as cool and unpretentious as her cut-off wetsuit, or her brown cords. Victoria was so beautiful it hurt.

Nathan had claimed that he was 'going to get into her' since day one of the trip, but it didn't seem likely.

I started to catch as many White Teat as Victoria on each dive. She was happy for me and my progress. She gave me tips on how to get better and wasn't threatened or concerned that I was as good as her.

I also worked out how to use the computer. It was pretty simple. It told me how deep I was and how long I had been down for. It beeped if you stayed down for too long, but usually we heard Barnes' enraged banging on the side of the boat before the computer became too concerned. When Barnes hit the side of the boat with his rubber mallet, the sound meant one thing for us: 'GET THE FUCK OUT OF THE PISS, YOU USELESS CUNTS!'

One afternoon, just before our last dive of the day, Barnes told us we were going to head home straight afterwards. I looked at my hands before I put on my worn-out gloves. They had turned into war zones from the daily handling of the cucumbers. Gutting sea cucumbers is as fun as it sounds, with the added bonus being that their insides are poisonous and disgusting. The 'slug juice' seemed to work like paint stripper on bare skin, and my hands were the worst affected—they were red-raw, like I'd taken an overhead mark with a flaming meteor. It would have made wanking difficult but I hadn't had an opportunity to try.

When we slashed open a sea cucumber, its guts spilled over the portable gutting table. In the case of 'elephant trunks,' occasionally more than guts came out. Living inside the toxic bodies of these bizarre creatures was an even more bizarre creature; a gut eel. Fuck knows how they got in there, but there they were, crawling around the table, wondering what the fuck happened to their house. They were about five centimetres long, with a massive skull. If they had the dimensions of a shark, they'd be really fucking scary-looking. I nearly shat myself when I saw one writhing around the table for the first time.

'What the fuck is that?' I asked.

'It's a gut eel, ay?' replied Stan.

'I guess it is, mate. If you say so.' Fucking Queensland hicks.

Before we could do anything, Nathan had grabbed the little, sperm-like creature and was rubbing it in the salt bin.

'Mmmmm, you like salt, don't you? Hey guys, look at this. I'm about to force feed it some salty goodness, like that Irish bitch that gobbed me in Townsville square.'

Stan walked purposefully around the table towards Nathan and a short scuffle resulted. In the commotion, the salt and the gut eel flew over the railing towards the ocean and freedom. Triumphant music burst from the sky, and the salt sprinkled the waves in slow motion and the heroic escapee hit the water and duck-dived into freedom.

'Don't do that again, ay?!'

'Why the fuck not?'

'Cos you just don't, ay? Got it, Nathan?'

'Well you're the fucking head diver so I'd better do what you say.'

'That's right, ay?'

From that point on, there was conflict between Nathan and Stan around the gutting table, especially when a gut eel burst out of its host. They'd both lunge for it with both hands; Nathan trying to kill it, Stan trying to save it. The eel was probably having enough problems adapting to its new surroundings without negotiating two giants grabbing at it. Usually in the commotion, the eel escaped.

Unbeknownst to the eels, they had started something that couldn't be stopped. Nathan Punt and Stan Dwyer really started to dislike each other. The eel scuffles became more and more heated, as did every exchange between them.

With red-sore hands and alcohol-deprived kidneys, it was time to clean up as many sea cucumbers as I could for one last time.

I geared-up slower than usual, like a footballer getting ready for a grand final. Fins on, mask on, weight belt on, stupid computer on my wrist, neck-bag around my neck. I waddled down the ladder into the water. Victoria helped me clip the big, yellow hose to my weight belt. I checked if the air was on by breathing through my regulator at the end of the yellow hose. It worked. It was time to swim out to my chain. Mine was always at the far end of the boom on the starboard side. Victoria's was always on my inside lane. Neville had the port side to himself.

I swam out to my chain, checking that the 'Big Bag' was attached properly to those tricky clips that were impossible to attach and detach. The big bag was like an unloading depot for the bag around my neck. When my neckbag was full, I would empty it into the big bag and keep diving. The boys on the last dive had come up with barely anything, so they hadn't needed to winch the big bags out of the water and onto the deck. There was nothing in them.

The bunch of chains hung about three metres beneath the surface. It looked like a robotic bunch of kelp. The big bag was roughly a metre above the chains, attached to the rope. Two metres above that was me, hanging on to the rope, waiting for the whole lot of us to drop.

Vwoosh

Dropping thirty-five metres in a matter of seconds was breathtaking every time. Once on the ocean floor though, it was all business. The visibility was good. I could see Victoria patrolling her area, and Neville kicking about in his own girlish way. The grounds looked good, and pretty soon it was slug-fucking-city. There must have been a White Teat convention going on, because there were too many to catch. I had to keep climbing back to the big bag to empty my neck-bag before heading back to the slug-fest. They were on the sand, they were in rocky ledges, and they were among the coral and on top of bommies. All three of us were cleaning up big time.

We were down there for twenty-five minutes. After about six minutes, I'd completely lost count of White Teat.

'So, Kelvin, what a fairy tale end to your sea cucumber diving trip. You must be happy to end on such a high,' I said to myself through my regulator, while still tearing through the White Teat.

'Yes, that's true, Kelvin. I always considered myself to be a good team player. At the end of the day, it's just good to get the score on the board.'

'So, anything to say to the knockers who didn't think you were up to scratch early on in your career?'

'No, I won't name names. People are entitled to their opinion, and I just hope that some opinions...'

Whack!

Fuck, I wasn't concentrating. Mid-interview, I drifted straight into a huge, tree-like coral. I smashed it into pieces with my head and shoulders, sending all of its then-homeless inhabitants swimming in all styles and directions. As I was trying to regain my composure, I was being grated, face-down, across the ocean floor. My neck-bag was heavily full of slugs, restricting my buoyancy. Still, I got my shit together and checked my air hose; it was fine. I looked around. Neville and Victoria hadn't even noticed what I'd done. It was as if that whole little episode had never happened. I decided not to return to the interview, and went back to cashing in on the slug smorgasbord in front of me. There were fucking millions of 'em!

When it was time to come up, Victoria and I went on a long oxygen hang. For twenty-five minutes, I looked deep into her eyes and dreamt away.

My tally would put me in second spot—second only to the Paul Hart machine. Nathan and Stan could suck on my bubbles. Those twenty-five minutes rocked. Victoria looked as hot as usual; simply irresistible. We were together, we were dive buddies. We had an invisible bond between us in the water. I could tell that she was thinking about me.

As I climbed back on board, I walked straight towards the captain.

'How much fucking slug did you catch?'

'Roughly 120, I suppose. I lost count.'

He looked neither surprised nor impressed.

'Did you lose that computer? Cos if you fucking did....'

I held my wrist up to him.

'You'll have to pay for it. So, where the fuck is it?'

'What the fuck?'

I looked at my wrist. It wasn't there. I checked the other wrist, and not there. I started looking madly around the deck and in my neck-bag. I jumped back into the water and searched through the big bag full of cucumbers. It wasn't anywhere.

Barnes walked up to me. I was expecting him to hit me, but he was actually more calm than usual.

'Look, old mate, we can work something out. Don't worry about it.'

Chapter Eleven

'Okay, boys, I've got the cheques for you here. They're good to go,' said Barnes at the dock. He had done all the paperwork during the twelve-hour steam back home.

'Most of you guys have made decent pay. You can't complain when you leave with over $1,500 for the trip. I'd take that every time, you cunts.'

It seemed that he had become much nicer during the last quarter of the trip. On the last day he even told a couple of racist jokes to liven things up.

The boys gratefully took their money from him. He didn't shake their hands, but he did look them in the eyes when he handed the cheques over. Then he looked straight at me.

'We'd better have a little chat, mate,' he said, glaring into me.

'The rest of you guys can fuck off now,' he concluded nicely, as he gestured towards the pier.

Barnes explained to me that I was in arrears. He produced a catalogue that showed how much it would cost him to replace the computer that I had lost. They were very expensive, just a touch over two grand. $2000! That was a lot of fucking beers, man. I had no money at all. If you then added the 560 bucks from the dive course, it hadn't been the most profitable outing.

'Well that's me fucked then, isn't it?' I asked.

'Like I said, we'll work something out.'

Barnes had me at his mercy. He didn't need to yell at me. He told me that I could live on the boat for the next week until the next trip went out. I could earn my rent by cleaning the boat and generally doing whatever the fuck Jesse Barnes wanted me to do. It was about my only option. I had worked harder than I ever had before in my life, all for the privilege of being boat-ridden until this God-awful ship went back out to sea again.

I watched from my new home as the guys walked along the pier towards freedom and the pub.

I climbed up to the top deck and repeatedly kicked a pile of ropes while muttering unpleasantries under my breath. Victoria interrupted me.

'Bummer about the dive computer.'

'Yes, it is. Generally I like being able to eat and live.'

'You'll be all right. It's not like you got the bends or anything.'

'I wish I had; at least I'd be getting food at the hospital.'

'Here,' she said.

Victoria placed a fifty-dollar note into my hand. Our hands stayed locked for a moment before she withdrew.

'Thank you,' I said.

'I just want to make sure you can eat for the next week. Go to Bi-Lo before you spend it anywhere else.'

And that is exactly where I was headed when I ran into Neville. He was sitting outside at P.J. O'Brien's.

'Comin' for a drink?'

'Yeah, all right. But, only one. I've got to go to the supermarket.'

The binge took hold of me from there.

I still had sea legs from the trip and I was drunk after the first pot. Neville was feeling good about his earnings and was shouting me rounds in between seething about our fair captain.

'It's like this, innit? I don't mind bein' told to do stuff different, right. But that guy is being a cunt for the sake of it, innit? I'd love to damage him.'

It wasn't long before I couldn't understand the guy. I smiled and laughed with him. What I could understand was that he was ending every sentence with 'I'd love to damage him, innit?' and it was getting more and more venomous every time.

It got dark, and the supermarket was forgotten. We went to the Sportsbar and I was drunk enough to want to dance. My clothes looked like crap and I was delirious, but I managed to pull some girl from the dance floor. She was a plump blonde from England. I can't remember her name.

'Do you want to see my boat, blonde English girl?'

It was on.

Barnes had only given me the keys to our cabin. Unfortunately, I couldn't fuck this chick on Barnes' desk in the wheelhouse, or on the kitchen table. Still, rooting is good. I had been unable to masturbate during the last nineteen days, and this chick was gonna pay for it in the cabin. I was rock hard and annoyed; she got it angrily all night.

Stan Dwyer's night

Geez, I was glad to get off that fucking boat and into some bourbons, ay? Those cunts, except for Nathan, are solid blokes, but you get sick of them up your dart all fucking day long, ay?

I was stoked we made it back for Sunday night, cos I got this gig lined up at the open mic night at the Green Ant Cantina. I was a bit nervous, ay? So I downed a few pots and a couple of bourbons before they called me up to do my comedy routine.

I took off my shirt off and started talking to the cunts in the crowd.

'Are there any Jewish lesbians here, ay?' I asked, and got no response.

'Cos if there are, come up on stage so I can punch youse in the cunt, ay?'

The crowd was pretty small and they weren't really getting into it, ay? So I do a few jokes about Katie Price's first son, Harvey. The cunts still didn't quite get it. They must have all been fucking poofs. When I said that shit to my mates over a few bourbons, they thought it was piss funny, ay?

So I fucked off offstage for a second and came back dressed as Al Kyder, the bumbling terrorist. In my best Middle Eastern accent I said, 'I'm gonna blow the fuck out of all youse cunts with my strap-on,' revealing a big fucking dildo coming out of my white robes.

That got a reaction, so I went with it and started chasing chicks in the audience with it, ay? Some of the cunts are laughed but the security guy didn't, and he sort of just kept me running out the door, ay?

After that I heard big applause, which I hoped was for me.

I went back to the hostel to dissect the fuck out of my performance, work on my act and drain a few bourbons. Maybe I have to stop with all of this politically correct bullshit next time, ay?

Nathan Punt's Night

I went to the common room of the International Hostel and started up a conversation with some English chicks. I pretended to be interested in what part of England they came from and laughed at their jokes. Then, without an invite, they said they were off, and they left.

I lost my mojo a long time ago. Some of the stories I tell are truthful, but they are mainly based around the shared adventures of me and my ex-wife. Yes, we were really young. Yes, when you are young and naïve, you think that it will last forever. But when she left me that day, she took a whole chunk of Nathan Punt with her.

I've got a photo of her in my wallet still. She is an impressive-looking lady and I used to stun people when I showed them the photo of my wife. I may have been punching above my weight, but, man, was I punching. Now the photo sits permanently next to a condom that must be a couple of years past its use-by date.

I finally went to The Sports Bar to see if I could garner some close companionship, or even friendship. I kept a lookout for any of the sea cucumber crew too, just in case they wanted to join me.

I didn't find anybody, so I sat at the extremely busy bar, and slowly drank my pay packet away. I spoke to nobody and eventually slunk off home.

Chapter Twelve

A week passed. I managed to get some cash out of Centrelink. It was enough to keep me in muesli bars and vodka. Barnes had huge plans for me. He had me scrape out vegetable matter from the floor of the refrigerator room. I had to get into a full box-jellyfish-proof ninja suit, jump into the shitty, everything-infested waters of Trinity Wharf, and scrub the sides of the Bêche De Mer. I had to clean out our cabin-cave, which was a pointless exercise. I was even sent to Barnes' backyard to feed that little, yappy, fur-ball every now and then. Not that Harlot was ever glad to see me, even if I was brandishing food. As a final insult, I had to pick up its shit in a plastic bag and throw it in the nearest dog-bin, which was thirty minutes' walk away.

Barnes, being Barnes, hadn't told me when we'd be heading out again. So, I was actually pleased when I saw the outlines of Neville and Stan coming towards me from the end of the pier.

'All right, innit?'

'G'day mate, ay?'

The two boys had been staying at the Paradise Hostel. I felt a small pang in my soul as I remembered the good old days of cleaning the occasional toilet and stealing pasta.

'How was that roundish slapper you pulled the other night, you dirty man-whore?' asked Neville.

Just then Barnes, Victoria, and Harlot appeared.

'Not a fucking word to either of them. You got that?'

'Sure,' yelled Neville, towards the end of the pier that Victoria and Barnes were approaching from. 'I WON'T SAY A THING ABOUT THAT BRITISH BINT YOU BROUGHT BACK ONTO JESSE BARNES' PRIVATE AND COMMERCIAL PROPERTY, AND FUCKED INTO NEXT TUESDAY, AFTER SPENDING ALL THE FOOD MONEY THAT VICTORIA SPARED YOU ON BEER!'

I was hoping that they were still out of earshot, but Barnes' face had gone from pink to scarlet, and his expression from angry to furious. He started squawking.

'WHAT THE FUCK IS GOING ON?! WHAT'S THIS GINGER CUNT TALKING ABOUT?! WHERE'S NATHAN PUNT?! WHERE'S PAUL HART?'

Arf, arf, arf, grrrrrrrrrr!

'WHAT THE FUCK ARE YOU GUYS DOING STANDING AROUND?!'

Grrrrrrrr ... arf, arf, arf!

'GET ON DECK! WE'VE GOT DORIES TO CLEAN AND SALT BAGS TO MOVE! C'MON!'

ARF, ARF, ARF, ARF, GRRRRRR!

At least he wasn't enraged about what Neville had said; he was just enraged about everything.

Nathan arrived just after that outburst. In a rare show of good sense, he started working quietly. Paul arrived so quietly that nobody noticed his presence until he'd been working for several hours.

Meanwhile, Captain Jesse Barnes sat in his wheelhouse, watching us like the Evil Emperor of the Obese Meerkats. When the mood took him, he opened the window to consult us on our projects. Neville seemed to be the most frequently consulted.

'Neville, what the fuck? You useless, pommy piece of shit! Why do you take twice as long as an Aussie to do sweet fuck-all?' he squawked.

'I'll tell you why that is, guv!' spat Neville, with fury in his squinting eyes.

'Fuck-up. You're a fucking disgrace, even for a Londoner. I bet your slut of a mother wished she took it up the arse when she was getting pounded by Daddy in the alleyway all those years ago!' Barnes replied.

Neville glared back at him, exasperated.

'What? You've got nothing to that? Hey!? Hey, you useless, pommy cunt!? WHAT HAVE YOU GOT TO SAY TO THAT?'

'I'm not originally from bleeding London, guv. I was born in Essex, innit?'

'IS IT JUST ME, OR DID THE WORLD GET MORE FUCKING BORING THEN, WITH YOU AND YOUR FUCKING LIFE STORY? YOU'RE A POMMY LONDONER, SO SHUT UP!'

Neville stood and stared at the wheelhouse, standing and staring at Barnes for an eternity. He was staring like a psychopath. He had a look of genuine hate, a look that was coming straight back at him from behind the perspex of the wheelhouse. Days of our lives came to mind; as the two of them looked at each other I could no longer tell if it was hate or love they had in their eyes.

After what felt like thirteen hours of this bullshit stand-off, Neville was the first to throw in his hand. He walked off, leaving Barnes looking even more smug than usual.

As Neville shuffled past me, I could hear him muttering the line, 'Right then, Jonny, let's go for it,' over and over.

Barnes triumphantly rose from his throne as if he'd won a heroic battle. His fat, gloating face reddened from the struggle of extricating his fat, gloating arse from his seat.

I was in the act of uselessly moving heavy barrels from one side of the boat to the other, paying homage to the Egyptian slaves who died before me. I didn't even know what was in the barrels. Neville strode towards me with a blank expression, stopping inches before my face.

'Look, guv, you're not a bad bloke an' that.' He paused, and grabbed my T-shirt and whispered, 'Just take care o' yourself, yeah?'

These were the only nice words I had ever received from Neville. In fact, I can't recall him saying anything good to anyone he didn't want to shag. His unusual behaviour had started to concern me—but not enough for me to act.

I kept my head down, concentrating on the importance of the duties delegated to me. As I stopped to take a breath, I looked across to see Harlot, standing on the back deck, looking back at me. She pondered me in silence. That expression of hers was usually followed by aggressive growling and barking. I prepared for the inevitable onslaught when I spotted Neville, hunched over, three metres away from the dog. His hands were cupped together in front of his chest, a thoughtful expression on his face. His stance and expression mirrored that of his idol, Jonny Wilkinson, lining up the uprights to put England in front of Australia in the World Cup finals.

He took one contemplative look outward and upward, towards some imaginary target, like he'd seen Jonny do a thousand times. He then took three fast and deliberate paces towards the oblivious, furry football.

The next part happened in slow motion. There was a distinct whoosh as Neville calmly but powerfully swung his left foot into Harlot's underbelly. There was a thud of bare foot hitting bare dog that sounds very similar to that of a football being kicked. The thudding sound was followed immediately with a surprised 'arf,' that was squeezed out of the lungs of the little canine. Harlot's expression was one of confusion as she started to take off. Triumph was written on Neville's face as Harlot flew from the middle of the front deck, soaring like a sugar glider towards the murky waters of Trinity Wharf.

Neville and I were the only people who saw what happened. The other boys were on the upper-deck, stacking boxes, under the supervision of Barnes. Victoria was out shopping for the trip.

We stood, stunned and silent.

Harlot hit the water and started whining in strained and painful sound-bites.

'WHAT THE FUCK?!' were Barnes' only words as he ripped off his singlet. His large belly rippled as he bolted down the ladder towards the edge of the boat. He launched himself over the railing of the vessel like a trained walrus. As he paddled out to save his beloved Harlot, I saw Neville standing on the pier, his bags packed and slung over his shoulders. He was wearing Barnes' $370 dollar Ray-Bans.

He called out to me.

'I'd better be 'eadin' out of Cairns then, innit guv?

'Do yourself a favour. Don't let that fat bastard back on to the boat.'

Neville then calmly turned around, and strutted along the pier towards the road, where a rank of taxis waited for him. He had an air of power and control that I had never associated with the man. After five seconds of looking cool, he broke into a frenzied sprint—similar to that of a twelve-year-old girl—along the pier, and out of my life.

The Jendaya Chronicle: Part Three

The four of us approached the fence. There were no animals around and it made me wonder why. Were they afraid of the fence? I was worried that bad people might be frightening all the animals away.

Mummy explained to us, in her own special language of English and Shona, that we had to climb over the fence to get away from Zimbabwe. I hadn't yet asked Mummy what was going on or where we were going. I think I didn't really want to know, in my heart, what had happened to our farm and our daddy. Mummy told me anyway.

'Zimbabwe is a country that is not fair for any human being. The money that we saved up over the many years by hard work is now worth nothing. Our farm was all that we had and still gave us the chance to live and keep you three children healthy. As you know, we all worked very hard together on this farm. But the man who worked the hardest was your father.'

She paused for the longest time, until the welling tears in her eyes could no longer be held back.

'Your father is dead.'

Deep down, we all knew this already. But at that moment we all wailed and moaned together as a family, in unified grief.

Eventually, I asked Mummy why Daddy had died and also asked where we were going. It took her a long while to respond, such was her sadness. She still looked from side to side along the fence the whole time.

'The government here does not like white farmers. They say that we should not be allowed to farm on any African lands. That is what those people with guns kept saying to us. They told us that we had to leave immediately. They also said that we were a filthy, mixed-race family that didn't belong in this wonderful country. "What do you mean 'wonderful'?" said your daddy. "I am trying to look after my wife and kids. I am causing no harm to anybody. I provide food for the people who live in Zimbabwe. This country is not wonderful."

'The men then said that we had to move out today, because other, real Africans were moving in. Daddy said that this was impossible, so they shot him in the head. They told me that we were now homeless and that I should take the children somewhere far away from the farm. They said that we were criminals who were guilty of trespassing. That is why we left home. This country and its politicians have betrayed us, so we are climbing over this fence to get to South Africa. We must hurry too. We don't want to get caught too close to either side.'

Emmi asked us why we didn't simply crawl through a hole in the fence that he had spotted. We all decided this was a good idea. Soon we had all climbed through the hole which looked like it had been used by many people before us. There was a beaten track that led away from the fence. We followed it, and it guided us to swampland. There were only two ways to go; either straight through the swamp or back to the fence. Mum told us that the only way to get to food and friendly people was to keep going through the swampland. So, we kept walking forward in the wet mud.

Soon, it wasn't just mud but also water that was getting quite deep. It came up to my waist which meant that it was nearly deep enough for the boys to have to swim in. We all knew how to swim because we had a big dam at our farm. Mummy told us to pretend that we were explorers and that we were looking for the lost world of Lollies. The boys loved it and started playing along. Emmi pointed at a tree and said that he had found a clue and started wading towards it. He was about two metres in front of Mummy and Jabi, when I saw a giant crocodile burst out of the water and grab Emmi's head in its mouth. He was pulled face first under the water. I saw a couple of splashes and then a long tail disappeared back into the brown liquid. That was the last time I saw my brother.

Mummy ran towards where Emmi was last seen. I grabbed Jabi, but there was nowhere to go. We stood still. Mummy dived into the water but couldn't find Emmi.

Eventually we kept wading, knowing that one of us could be killed at any time without warning. Nobody cried because we were too scared for ourselves. Soon ,the water became less deep; we could see the crocodiles and steer clear of them. So we walked and walked onward in silence. Jabi was lost without his twin brother. We were all lost and scared without poor Emmi.

We travelled in our wet clothes for hours and hours, until the swamp turned back into dry desert. We walked out into the baking sun. Our wet, dirty clothes turned into dry, muddy clothes. There was no shade, and there were no people. I wanted to lie down and sleep forever, but Mummy kept telling us to keep walking. We all kept walking. When Jabi collapsed, we stopped.

He was very sad about his brother and was feeling very hot and tired. He could no longer walk, so we all stopped and lay down in the burning sun. It felt wonderful to break and relax. In my dream, I was warm and safe. When I woke up, it was getting dark and cold. We got up and started walking again to keep the cold away from us. It worked. On and on we walked for days. I kept a lookout, although I didn't know what for, until we found a cricket oval that was full of people.

The town was called Musina. Although there were thousands of people, there was no food or shelter for us.

My mum, my brother and I were starving to death, when I met a man. He offered my family food and water. We accepted the food and water, and then he took me by the hand to his building. He told my Mummy and my brother to wait outside. I never saw them again.When I think of my family, I think of love and happiness. I miss them.

Chapter Thirteen

I wish I'd had the balls to pull off a stunt like that.

After retrieving his dog and rushing her to the vet, Jesse Barnes tried to track down Neville, who, I assume, had left the state and possibly the country.

When Barnes returned, he worked what was left of his labour force with more hatred and anger than usual.

After a few more hours of pointless barrel moving and deck scrubbing, he called us in together for a meeting.

'Right, you cunts, this is what's happening. We leave tonight at seven o'clock. Because of that little shit-head and his murderous actions, we are a diver short. It looks like I'll be jumping into the piss with you guys.'

I wished that Jesse Barnes had been simultaneously attacked by crocodiles, sharks and Harlot while he was in the water.

'Now, I'll have you know that I'm fucking good, so you'll have to do your fucking best to keep up with me.'

The day dragged on. The sun shone, the barrels got heavier, Barnes squawked, and life pretty much went back to normal. Eventually, Victoria returned from the vet with the news that Harlot wasn't dead and that she was as perky and feisty as usual at the kennels. Barnes was still fucking angry, and he directed his rage at us. He told us that if we saw, heard, or even thought about Neville's whereabouts we were to tell him, or we were fucked. The sun got hotter, and we kept working.

At seven, we untied the ropes and set off to the Coral Sea.

The sea was rough.

The boat shirt-fronted each wave with aggression.

For the whole two-and-a-half days that we were steaming out to Holmes Reef, I was seasick. I rarely talked. I slept even less, and I didn't eat. Victoria was cooking delicious-smelling meals that I couldn't touch.

There is no hiding from seasickness.

For most of the first day I was spewing up orange, chunky vomit. It had a rancid odour that clogged my sinuses and an aftertaste that clung to the back of my throat.

I didn't think that my stomach could offer any more to the ocean. After twelve hours the vomit had become just bile, which had the consistency and colour of a weakly mixed cordial. By day two, it was barely yellow anymore; it was a cloudy, see-through liquid. It got boring being doubled over at the edge of the boat, using all my weight and strength to force out the smallest amount of ghost water.

All day, all night, staring at the ocean moving beneath the boat, involuntarily forcing my will-to-live out of my face.

The guys on the boat didn't seem to care much. They kept away from me, which was good. I avoided Victoria as much as I could. I'm not sure what women want but I'm pretty sure they don't want guys with tears in their eyes and stomach-lining cascading out of their nostrils.

'Isn't it funny how you always have carrots in your chuck? I mean, I've never eaten carrots in my life, but, sure enough, when I hurl, there they are. What's with that?' observed Nathan, while I was bent over on the back deck. He had his 'Nathan Punt is a legend' look on his face.

'Punt, I've never heard that before. You are so original. You should be a comedian, because I really, really, haven't heard that ever before.'

'Yeah, I guess that was a pretty good call.'

Nathan didn't understand sarcasm. In fact, if Nathan did understand anything you said, chances were he wasn't listening. He only heard what he wanted to hear.

A conversation with Nathan typically went something like this:

'Hey Nathan, while I was on that last dive I saw a pack of killer whales circling around a giant squid. They were about to attack it before I intervened.'

'Yeah? One time I rooted this chick on a pool table and my mate filmed it with his mobile phone.'

Once we finally made it into Hollinson Reef, things were not so hard to deal with. The water was calm, being protected from the thrashing ocean by the coral framework of the reef. My seasickness had subsided. My stomach and I were friends again.

Even Nathan had gone momentarily quiet as if he too was controlled by the waves. The only reason I knew we were inside a reef was because Barnes had told me—'We're in the fucking reef,' to quote the man exactly.

It must have been a big reef, because the blue, flat, sheet of water on which we were sitting extended out to each and every horizon, with no obstacles in sight.

I wished it was just me and Victoria.

Neville Lives On

Even I was impressed with my departure from Cairns. I could see my balls growing in the minds of all parties concerned, innit? I don't like cruelty to animals or nuffin, but sometimes if you want to make an omelette you gotta kick a few dogs.

I 'it the frog and toad quick, and was 'oping to get to Airlie Beach but ran out of money in Tully, which is a fucking stones-throw from fucking Cairns, innit? There is this giant Golden Gumboot in the middle of town where the bus dropped me, and a park.

I was kind of 'anging about the park for a bit, when a group of about six Aborigines asked me if I wanted to hang out with them. I said fuck yes, as I was way too close to Jesse Barnes and wanted to be surrounded at all times.

I 'ad a bit of pot with me, and 'aving 'eard that they are community-minded people, I sparked up a joint and shared it around.

Even though we were in a park in the middle of a town, nobody gave a shit that we were smoking illegal drugs in public. It was weird, cos if I tried that in Cairns or in Bristol, I'd get banged up for the night.

One of the older guys noticed me looking all about the place and asks me who is after me. Pure genius, innit? He didn't have to ask any preliminary questions, just straight the facts.

So I tell them the story of my Trinity Wharf incident, and they are all amused and well fucking impressed. The women started looking at me differently after the story too.

On the spot, they invite me to stay with them until I sort myself out enough to 'ead south. On the spot, I accept. These people are fucking classic geezers that I could learn from, so we 'ead off to wherever they live.

Chapter Fourteen

Before I had time to ponder too much on things we'd been out at Hollinson reef for a week. The entire operation was completely different from the last trip. We actually had to read and listen to our computers 'cause we were diving off the little dories that we'd dragged behind the Bêche De Mer all the way out there. I took extra special care to not drop my computer.

Three of us went out at the start of each day in one of the two dories. Usually, Barnes took Nathan and Stan in the good dory, with a steering wheel, shelter, and a general degree of comfort. That left myself, Paul 'Personality' Hart and Victoria to take out the appropriately christened Piece Of Shit—or POS, as we called it. That was fine with me, cos I got to spend time alone with Victoria—Paul didn't really count as a person. The diving had become automatic for me:

Survey the reef.

Start at the bottom.

Patrol left, patrol right.

Crane up the reef.

Pick up the White Teat.

Keep moving.

Dodge the sea snake.

Keep moving.

Beep, beep, goes the computer.

Go up a few metres.

Keep patrolling.

Catch the cucumbers.

Fill the bag, then send it home.

Keep moving.

Keep patrolling.

Make sure that none of them get away.

NONE WILL BE SPARED (except the really small ones).

Eventually the little computer would start going mental and I'd come up to the surface, depriving the reef of all its sand-filterers along the way.

Our boat was consistently bringing in more slugs than the other boat. Vic and I were both good, but the Hart-man was quite unbelievable. He inflated the balloons of two full bags at the one time and sent them up to the POS via his long air-hose with amazing regularity. By the time we were finished dealing with them, another two would be floating at the surface. Victoria looked puzzled after a while, as if he might be cheating down there.

On the ninth day, our crew came back to the main boat slightly earlier than usual. Paul Hart had come out of the water with his usual bag-loads of slugs in the early afternoon; it was too late to go for another dive. But it was still a risk to go back to our main quarters early. If Barnes saw us coming in at that time, he'd go off his flabby tits at us. We took a chance and headed into the Beche De Mer.

We counted and processed our catch quickly and quietly. Hart, by example, commanded efficiency, speed, and very little conversation. He disappeared once we'd finished. He seemed to dissolve into water quite regularly.

For the first time, Victoria and I had a bit of time alone out of the water. We sat on the top deck and chatted, gazing out to sea. There was no sign of Barnes and his harmonious, micro-crew.

'Victoria,' I said. 'How is it that you found yourself in this line of work?'

She paused and exhaled, as if smoking an invisible cigarette. Her blonde eyebrows and forehead, still glistening wet from the salt water, furrowed. She looked at her small, white hands for a while, and then folded her arms and looked out to the sea.

Finally, she spoke.

'It's complicated.

'To start with, my uncle doesn't treat me like he treats the rest of you guys. Because I'm the chef, I get paid much better than you do. I won't have to do this for much longer, and I'll have enough money to travel to Europe.'

'I don't really belong out here with these guys,' she said, 'and neither do you.'

'Don't you think?'

'No, you don't. You are not a very good catcher,' she said bluntly. 'But, it's not just that. You are too smart to be out here with guys like Nathan Punt and Stan Dwyer.'

She looked at me earnestly with her ocean-blue eyes. Flecks of hazel swirled through her beautiful retinas.

'Really?' I said, sounding as daft as an unscripted George W after three bongs and a tequila slammer.

'Yeah. Those guys have got their stories and their little worlds, and that is fantastic. But I just don't picture you being like them. You are different, Kelvin.'

Again, she looked straight at me. Her features were so soft and beautiful, it hurt.

'Believe me, this is my last trip,' I decided then and there.

'And then what, Kelvin?'

'I've been thinking of doing my dive instructor's course and then maybe travelling,'

I decided then and there.

'Maybe we should head to Amsterdam together.'

'Amsterdam?'

'Yeah, it's the most liberal city in the world. You can do anything and be anyone in Holland. You should come with me. We'll have so much fun, and you can keep doing diving training.'

'So, are we going to Holland or Amsterdam?'

'We can go to both, Kelvin. I think that you'll need me to look after you in Europe.'

Whatever her reasoning, it sounded brilliant.

'Well, you can look after me if you want, but I can reciprocate, you know?'

Wow, I was flirting. And we were talking about a future off the boat.

Real travelling.

With Victoria.

This could be good.

We made a pact. After the trip, we'd save the money somehow and hightail it out of this hemisphere.

Then we stared, not out at the sea, but deep into each other's eyes. I was trying to look calm, but internally I was freaking out. I'm not good in these situations at the best of times. But when I'm sober? Fucking hell. I had no idea what the fuck I was supposed to do next. So I kept staring, with a stupid half-grin on my face. Usually when I look at her, I start picturing her naked on all fours. But not that time. That time, I took in all of her features, and appreciated exactly how stunning she was.

Her wet hair was in a gorgeous-yet-practical pony tail. Her eyes were trying to swallow me up.

We stared at each other for fucking ages. I'm sure she was expecting me to do something. It was set to go on for days, when the distant roar of an outboard motor broke the spell.

'I'd best be getting dinner sorted,' said the perfect one, and disappeared.

Missives Of Merpeople

Head Squihhsbah,

As you know, I have been working under the guise of a sea cucumber diver for two land-dwelling years. By convincing the captain that I was his niece, I have been able to gain information from both land and the ocean about the target. I was hoping, in time, that I would learn of his whereabouts, but it seems that he has come directly to me.

It is almost certain that I have found him. The target sticks out like a merman amongst humans. His underwater prowess is near super-human and his social skills limited.

I have been able to feel some of the missives he has sent back to his sect and to his father. His mission is very open and vague, but he still poses a threat to your plans.

His description matches the one given to you by his father, although of course he is in land-dwelling form. Despite his lack of social skills, the other crew members do not suspect him of being from the ocean.

So far, he does not suppose me to be one of his own. Be assured, he will be disposed of discreetly before he finds out too much. This will send a strong message to the sect and to the wider mer-community.

After that, I am to retire to Lake Ijmeer in Holland. I am looking forward to some rest and play within the wet dykes of Amsterdam. Thank you in advance for paying me promptly. I trust my tracking and killing skills have helped you keep the world in order.

The Merhunter

Chapter Fourteen Continued

As the good dory came closer, I could only make out two of the figures in the boat. They were standing, their bodies rigid and urgent. Their little craft raced over the water. In a matter of minutes they were tied up at the side of the Beche De Mer.

Nathan and Stan stood, while Barnes lay down.

'Barnes is fucked! Give us a hand, ay?!' yelled Stan. 'Fucking get out here and help us Kelvin!'

Now was not the time for a hearty round of applause, which is what I initially thought he was getting at. I ran to the port (or starboard—the left side, anyway) of the Beche De Mer and looked down into Barnes's dory. He was down and most certainly out. His limp body flobbed in the middle of the small vessel. His usual red glow was replaced by a grey indifference. His stout chest was barely rising and falling at all.

'We need to get him back on board and on pure oxygen,' yelled Stan. I jumped down into the dory. Victoria was nowhere.

'He's been bent, badly,' said Nathan.

'It doesn't fucking matter, ay? What matters is he is fucked, ay? Right, let's lift him up, ay? Now!' ordered Stan.

That was difficult. Barnes was a big weight, and the three of us heaved and grunted as we picked up his limp carcass. We hadn't thought too much about our next move, because we stood there holding him up like three pallbearers, with no real idea what to do. We couldn't really throw him two metres over the railing, could we? So, we stood there, supporting Barnes like a chariot, awaiting Stan's next order. The sea, like us, wasn't calm anymore. Balancing in the little boat, carrying a fleshy petrol-bowser on our shoulders was not easy. The dory kept tipping from one side to the next, and the more we tried to correct it, the more it to'd and fro'd. All the while we yelled out for Paul and Victoria, as loudly and angrily as we could.

Then I slipped over.

As I fell, I lost grip of Barnes's legs. I fell off the dory on the starboard (I think) side. From the water, I looked up just in time to see Barnes' groin falling straight onto my head.

CRACK!

There was blackness and quiet, then tranquil blue. Then there was red, red water all around me. I swam in the red mist: a beautiful crimson hue of love and lust.

A muffled voice sounded at me from beyond the red dimension. I looked up and saw a light, kind of like the sun, but more beautiful. I swam towards the amber light overlooking my world, hoping to find the voice that was summoning me. I never got to the amber light, because when my head burst from the red liquid, I saw Nathan and Stan looking frantically at the side of the dory.

'BARNES IS SINKING, AY?! CAN YOU GET HIM?' enquired Stan, loudly.

Fuck. Barnes. I'd forgotten all about him. After quickly surveying the scene, I realised I was in the middle of a big puddle of blood. It wasn't my blood though; it was that of our honourable skipper. He must have cut himself on the side of the dory on his way out. I was concussed enough to want to save the man.

'I'll get him. Chuck me a mask and fins now,' I demanded.

Stan did just that. Once I had quickly put on the gear, I checked under the water to see where he'd toddled off to. I was able to locate him by following the red trail. He was floating about three metres below the surface of the water. He wasn't going deeper or shallower; he was just levelling off, like a good scuba-diver should. It's called neutral buoyancy.

It struck me was that the guy was beyond saving. The fucker was dead, big time. A steady ray of blood beamed out from above his right eye. His body and face were limp. I duck-dived down, grabbed him by the hair, and dragged him back to the water's surface. I did a quick head-check to locate the Beche

De Mer and then swam slowly towards the boat, towing Barnes by his grey locks. My indifference towards Barnes enabled me to be calm, careful and not too bothered about rushing, until I saw the shark's fin.

I knew it was a Tiger Shark coming our way. I had never seen one, but there was no way that giant was a reef shark. During the trip I had heard plenty about them and their opportunistic ways, mainly from Barnes. It was fucking big and I could see its grey-striped body coming towards us.

Now, from what I had learned in my short diving career, sharks are good swimmers—much better swimmers than humans. I blocked out the yelling that was coming from the boat and tried to think. I had narrowed my options down to two:

Option one: I could swim back towards the boat, leaving Barnes floating.

Pros: I could possibly make it back in time, especially if the shark inspected Barnes first.

Cons: My splashy swimming style would most probably attract the shark's attention. If they could smell fear, I was reeking of it.

Option two: Stay very, very still, and hope that it went away.

Pros: That would require little physical activity and effort.

Cons: It could take a long time before I either got to safety or got my legs dined on.

I did neither and instead opted to do a little nervous Irish jig that moved me nowhere. The water shimmered as the shark approached us. I shoved Barnes towards the beast, like a pagan's offering to the god of the ocean. A huge impact shoved me five metres closer to the boat, and more blood stained the water. It was still not my blood, though. Barnes had been ripped out of my grasp, and I bolted for the Beche De Mer. The Tiger Shark must have been happy with Barnes and his energy-giving fat content, because I managed to get on board safely. Once safe, I looked out ten metres east (or left, or starboard) and watched as Barnes was systematically mauled by the Tiger Shark. Within minutes there were three Tiger Sharks in the area, along with several reef sharks. Eventually, a big turtle joined in the gnashing, biting, free-for-all. Finally, a menacing flock of Masked Boobies swooped in to finish off the bits.

We all looked on in silence. Victoria had returned from the kitchen to a surreal scene. Nobody spoke.

'Hey guys, I heard some shouting. What is going on?' asked Paul, who had also just appeared, looking clean-shaven and relaxed.

'Barnes is dead.' I said to Paul, Victoria and the horizon.

The Jendaya Chronicle: Part Four

The man, who never told me his name, put me in a room with other girls who were a similar age to me. I was fifteen years old, and had been looking forward to my birthday, which was still six months away. It didn't matter now.

The man was nice to me. He told me to eat and then rest.

We were provided with food, water and shelter, but this was at a great price. In exchange for these things I had always taken for granted, we were expected to deal with the many men that came to this big, tin shed.

I do not know how long I lived in this tin shed, but I was raped many times daily. It seemed like it was years. If we ever looked scared or fought back, the man, or one of his friends, would threaten to beat us or kill us. The man and his friends would point guns at us and hit us with phone books to keep us scared.

Some nights one of the girls would simply disappear and a new girl would be in her bunk bed the next morning. We were all too afraid to talk to each other, and I can't remember ever sleeping. All I remember are the thousands of shameful, angry men who violated my body and spirit every day and night.

I thought of my parents and my brothers, who were probably all together again now. The pain of the loss of my family was somehow comforting: it overrode the pain heaved into me by the horrible men. I would picture Jabi and Emmi playing on the farm, or Mummy and Daddy helping each other out in the kitchen. Over time, though, I could not picture my family being happy. Jabi and Emmi would stop playing and look at me disappointed; Mummy and Daddy would stop cooking and sigh. I realised that I either wanted to join my family for all eternity, or try to do something that would make them less disappointed in me. By trying to escape, I would realise one of these fates.

The shed looked like a very difficult place to escape from. The room that we were trapped in only had one door and this door was always guarded by the man, or one of his friends. The men always had big guns with them. I had never seen them use these guns on us but they always looked like they wanted to. As much as I tried, I could not remember how I was led into the horrible room of bunk-beds and, therefore, did not know how to get out.

Before I decided to escape, not paid any attention to anything in our living quarters. Once I had decided I was going to make a break for it, it became very important to me. If I was to succeed, I needed to look at my surroundings.

There was little to encourage me. There were no windows and no natural light. There were some light globes dangling from the ceiling that looked to be miles and miles above us. The walls that enclosed our room went nearly all the way to the ceiling, and the metal was too straight and slippery to climb. I could hear when one of the horrible customers came into the building and you could hear the men discussing money between each other, sometimes arguing, sometimes hitting each other. It was good that they were not always united. Sometimes when a fight started between the men, the man who was guarding us would leave his post for a minute to help sort it out.

I was usually too scared to try to escape during these moments, but now I had realised if I didn't escape or die, my short life would be spent in this room, dreading the times when I would be set upon in front of all the other poor girls.

I waited for weeks, or maybe months, for a fight to break out beyond our room. It was quite difficult to keep an eye on the guard without looking suspicious. The last thing I wanted to do was get the attention of one of them. I had seen the guards be horrible to some of the other girls for doing less than looking at them.

At last, my chance came. For some reason the men were shouting at each other again, this time not in English, or any language that I could understand. The man that was guarding our exit walked off, looking angry. He had left a small gun next to his chair, so I picked it up and sneaked out of the room, never to look back.

Our prison was the only room in the whole shed, it seemed. The rest was a big open area with a concrete floor, with a couch or table here or there. Lots of men were standing in a circle yelling at each other, with guns in their hands. They all looked very angry and nearly ready to use their weapons.

There was a big, open doorway on the other side of the circle of men. They looked distracted, but not distracted enough for me to sneak by unnoticed. I pointed the gun at the circle of men and then I pulled the trigger as many times as I could. It worked. Some of the men fell down straight away. The other men didn't know where the bullets were coming from, so they kept shooting each other until everybody, except me, was dead.

I took three of the handguns that looked the same as the one that I used, and found a stash of the bullets that came out of them. I also went through all of the dead men's wallets until I had quite a lot of money. Just before I went out the doors, I yelled to the other girls that they were free to leave now.

It was a bright day, which I had not seen for a lifetime, and I did not know where to go, or what to do. I had money, but I did not know where I could spend it.

I decided to walk. I walked through a neighbourhood of strangers staring at me until I found a main road, and I kept walking. I did not know which direction I was headed, or where I was next going to find shelter. I only sought to get away from that horrible place.

Soon a car stopped in front of me and a man told me to get in the car. I did as he said and he asked me where I wanted to go. 'Out of Africa,' I told him, and I pointed one of my guns at him.

He told me he didn't know how he could drive out of Africa, so I told him that he must try, or I would kill him. As it turned out, he drove me a long, long way before the petrol ran out, and then I killed him. I then took all of the money out of his wallet and started walking again.

Chapter Fifteen

'This is completely fucked up, ay?' said/asked Dwyer.

He had called a boat meeting in the lower galley, which we all attended, save for Victoria. She had returned to her room and couldn't be persuaded to come out.

'First, youse shouldn't get all fucked up about dropping Barnes, ay?'

'Well, I didn't drop him. It was you two,' accused Nathan, helpfully.

'Look, the cunt was bent and drowned by the time we got him back, ay? He was barely breathing, ay?' said Stan. 'I checked his dive computer and the cunt had been diving way beyond the limits. That's not our fault, ay?

'So'se, I'm the new skipper. First up, are youse cunts all right, or are youse still fucked up 'bout stuff?'

'I'm fine.'

'Sweet.'

'I'll be right.'

'Hated him.'

'Yeah, we all did, ay?'

The group murmured agreement, and silence descended.

'The satellite phone isn't working, ay?'

Another long silence was broken by Nathan. 'Who broke it?'

'That's not the fucking point, now, is it?' I interjected. 'The point is, that we have no way of contacting anyone, do we?'

'I'm just saying that I'm going to pound the living shit out of whoever broke the phone.'

'Well, that would achieve a lot. That would move us forward so many steps.'

'I know, mate, I know. So, who did it!?'

Fucking idiot.

'Listen, ay? The phone works orright. It's just that there's a code on the cunt-of-a-thing, ay?'

'Do you know it?'

'No, ay?'

'Well, I guess you don't know it if you said you don't,' I chipped in to confuse Stan.

'Ay?'

'Maybe he kept it in his room,' Paul bravely suggested.

'Yeah, but it's locked, ay? He's garn locked it with a padlock, with another code, ay?'

Crack.

Nathan walked from the table, took three paces towards the ex-captain's cabin door, and kicked it in with one mighty boot.

'Maybe, if we look through his stuff, we can find the code for the phone,' said a proud Nathan Punt. 'At least we can look through his stuff. I always wondered what was in here.'

'Yeah, me too,' chorused the rest of us, except Paul Hart, who returned to his role as a silent observer.

So, we switched the light on and had a look inside the ex-Barnes' ex-cabin. It was bigger than our cabin, and had two bunk beds. The top bunk had his sleeping bag and pillows on it.

'Hey, check it out,' said Nathan, opening a chest of drawers. He held up a bottle of Smirnoff vodka, and started swigging out of it. 'This is liquid panty removal.'

'Give that here.' I said, lunging at him. 'I'll take my panties off right now, if you want.'

'Easy, you big homo.'

'You know you want some of this,' I said, grabbing my crotch.

'Youse cunts will end up like Barnes if you keep acting like fags, ay?'

'Well, Nathan will end up just like Barnes if he keeps me from that bottle for a second longer.'

'Is this unusual?' inquired Hart quaintly, pointing towards the floor. He had removed the mattress from the bottom bunk to see if there were any keys or codes hidden there. He found no keys or codes, but he did find a shit-load of drugs.

There were dozens of vacuum-sealed bags filled with marijuana, pills and white powder. The inside of the bed was filled. It was a junky's slop-trough. Awesome.

'Fucken ay.'

'Yeah.'

'Fucken oath.'

'Give me that bottle right now!'

After everyone calmed down, we sat down at the table to discuss what we should do next. After an hour or so of discussion, we decided that the most mature and responsible plan would be this:

We would have to drive the boat home ourselves, as soon as possible. The fact that we were laden with drugs meant that Barnes may have had people to meet out here, people who might not be very nice. Also, because the phone was locked, we couldn't call for help, regardless. Captain Stan Dwyer claimed to be able to drive the thing, so that was good enough for us.

As for the drugs, we would take as many as we could on the way home. Once at our destination of Cairns, we would declare the remainder to the authorities.

We would also have to explain to the authorities why we were missing our captain.

'He got bent, drowned, and attacked by a shark, officer,' would be our stock reply. Telling the truth would make our story easy to remember.

So, that was our foolproof plan. Brilliant, hey? Nothing could possibly go wrong, if I could just get that fucking bottle of vodka out of Nathan's grasp.

Soon after that, I was feeling really, really good, man. The stars were glistening. Barnes was up in the sky, with all his evilness and obesity left behind in the mortal world. He was simply love. He was smiling down at me, and I'm pretty sure that the ecstasy was kicking in.

Robert Palmer was playing loudly and proudly in my soul, and I could feel his presence. His raspy vocals were wrapping around my body like a suave embrace. I could hear his message. I had been listening to him for months, but I never actually heard the message. His message was one of unity, strength and togetherness. Nathan, Stan, Victoria, Neville, Barnes, Harlot, Paul.

We were friends.

Family.

United.

One.

The black ocean kept disappearing under the boat. Love was all around. I could not wait to get home to spread my message. Things were going to be all right. No, they would be 'Simply Irresistible.'

I yelled out to the sea as loud as I could: 'YOU ARE SIMPLY IRRESISTIBLE!'

I was referring to the ocean, and death, and life. I found it overwhelming. And then I danced. I danced without air guitar, without fear, without inhibition. I moved my body to the essence of Robert Palmer. Undulating, swaying, and jumping to the atmosphere. Myself and the music of life were no longer two separate entities. We were one, and it was fun. I was happy.

'You know that I wrote "Simply irresistible" when I was your age.'

I turned around to see where the voice had come from. It didn't sound like any of the boys. It was gravelly and not Australian.

How I hadn't noticed him standing there before, I don't know. He was smoking a cigarette, standing slightly in the shadows. He was in a flawless, black suit; crisp, white shirt, golden cufflinks and blood-red tie.

'I wrote it about my future wife.'

Yep, it was the man himself. Robert Palmer. He was standing right at the front of the boat, near the anchor. Amazingly, his suit had not a trace of sea spray on it.

'Did she like the film clip?' I asked.

'Kelvin,' he said, 'I can't be here for very long, so listen.'

'Sorry, go on,' I said.

'Kelvin, the future for you can be a very bright one. You have to follow your needs and not your wants. You want to get wasted all the time. You want to spend all your money in this pursuit. Do you need this?'

'Well, I guess that in some ways—'

He cut me off. 'Kelvin, that was a rhetorical question. The answer is so evident that it needs no answering.'

'Sorry, mate, it's just that you paused when you asked. Also, I think that you'll find a rhetorical question is one that can't be answered, not one that's too fucking obvious to bother with,' I blurted out.

'That is wrong, but I am not here to argue. You need to take my advice. Since I died, I've seen your type—

I know what could be in store for you. So please, for your own sake, listen.'

'Sorry, Bob.'

'Don't worry about it, and don't ever call me Bob.'

He paused, and drew on his cigarette.

'Your journey in life has led you to this point. Soon, there will be a crossroad waiting for you. The path you take will decide your future. Choose the right path.'

He flicked his cigarette into the water, and another one appeared magically in his hands.

'Rob, mate,' I asked. 'Can you tell me about those voices and talking birds that have been fucking with my head lately?'

'We are all part of the same force, and don't call me Rob. Nothing we have said has been designed to hurt. We are here to help. Choose the right path, and we will observe from afar in admiration. We will have no need to talk to you in the physical realm ever again.'

'But how will I know what to do?'

'When it is time to choose, you will know,' he said. As he was talking, he was slowly starting to fade away in front of me. That dismayed me. It was too soon. There was still so much I wanted to know.

'Please don't give me that cryptic shit! Just tell me what to do. Do you actually know what is going to happen?'

'Pretty much.'

'Then why can't you tell me?'

'As a spirit guide, I can only lead you to a certain extent. I cannot control your destiny. Only you can. Think about it for a while.'

I pondered.

'Palmy. Mate, how many of those girls in your film clips did you shag?'

'Not that many. Auditioning them was fun, though. Call me Mr. Palmer,' he whispered. He was a transparency, and his voice was nearly muted.

'Hey, Robbo. What was it like to sing with UB40?'

'Dull.'

And he was gone. He had disappeared into the night from which he had sprung. Feeling drained, I located my bunk and fell asleep.

I woke up fuck-knows-when later. It was probably not that long. The chemicals in my body were not going to let me sleep anymore. I leaped out of bed and climbed up the ladder of the shitty, cramped bedroom that I'd come to know as home. I was still well-fucking wired and needed to do something, find someone, to interact, or, anything!

I walked laps around the boat for a while, looking out towards the horizon, hoping to find something exciting out there.

After possibly hours of circling and staring in anticipation, I stopped. The realisation of the ridiculousness of my actions suddenly dawned on me. I still had no idea what time it was. Checking the sky, I saw that it was starting to get a little less dark, but that didn't help me a whole lot.

Think Kelvin, think. What would Mr Palmer want you to do? Make the right choice.

Bingo! I should talk to whoever was doing the watch at the moment. Woo-hoo! I raced through the upper galley and into the wheelhouse.

'How the fuck are you doing, my main man!?' I exclaimed as I jumped around the corner, hoping to surprise whoever was on watch.

Silence. There was nobody in the wheelhouse. Not a soul. No people, birds, ghostly visions. Nobody.

I checked our recently written list, and guessed that it should have been Paul Hart on watch. It wasn't me, thank fuck, as I was only on during daylight.

Regardless of who should have been on watch, it looked like I was the man for the job. I had found something to do after all. I didn't really mind. I couldn't sleep and was pretty stoked that we hadn't run into any other ships or whales while the driver's seat was completely empty.

After ten minutes, I went to take a piss off the side of the boat. It was so very liberating. It then started to get light.

On the way back to the wheelhouse I noticed the peaceful figure of Paul Hart passed out under the table in the upper galley. He was on his back and was breathing with his trademark, quiet efficiency. He had an unwakeable look about him, so I decided to let him stay where he was. Still, I felt obligated to build a small monument of salt and pepper shakers, food tins, plastic chairs, and coffee mugs around his chest and face, for him to deal with when he woke up.

I was still feeling pretty good about everything. I put Rage Against the Machine into the CD player and started banging my head, yelling out the few words that I knew to each song. You could tell that the sun was just about to come up from beneath the sea. The sea was as flat as Justine Henin-Hardenne's chest, making sickness an improbability.

Splash!

A lone dolphin came closer and closer to the boat. Soon it became apparent that it wasn't alone. It was leading a whole troop of dolphins. There were heaps of them.

The whole boat was surrounded by these smarter relatives of the human race. The water was white and grey with splashing dolphins as far as I could see.

The sun had just started rising over the congregation, smiling in approval. I decided that I should wake up Nathan and Stan. Looking back, I should have just sat back, chilled out, and enjoyed the beauty of the moment. But I was still in a bit of a drug-love-daze, and wanted the guys to be part of it.

I swung the metal door of the cabin open and exclaimed, 'Get up guys, something awesome is happening.'

'Fuck off,' came the simultaneous response; a rare moment of unity between the two of them.

'Guys. The ocean is full of dolphins. It's awesome.'

'Right,' said Nathan. 'If you don't fuck off right now, I'm gonna kill you in front of your mum right before I fuck her brains out.'

'How many dolphins, ay?' asked Dwyer.

'Fucking thousands. Come have a look.'

'No worries, mate, ay?'

Stan jumped off his top bunk, making the loudest noise he possibly could. Nathan took a swipe at his leg, but missed. Dwyer responded by turning the lights on as he climbed up the ladder and slammed, and I mean fucking slammed, the door shut.

'So there's thousands of dolphins, ay?' he drawled, looking out into the ocean.

'Man,' I said apologetically, 'they were just here before. I swear.'

'You're a fucking mad cunt, ay?'

'Yes, I guess I am. But they really were here,' I went on. 'And, I think that you and Nathan should just chill out and relax about each other. Chillax! Just fucking take it easy before we get home. Karma guys, karma.'

'Nathan Punt can go get fucked,' he said, 'and so can youse for getting me up to see a thousand versions of sweet fuck all, ay?'

He took an aggressive look at everything and stormed back into the cabin, muttering something about 'fucking Melbourne trippers' under his breath. The hatch clanged shut as he pulled it with all his might behind him.

For the next two hours I sat in the wheelhouse. I plotted our course and checked for ships. In the many in-between moments, I considered how sane, if at all, I was. The drugs might be able to explain Mr Palmer but I didn't want that. I wanted him and his mysterious advice to be real. What about the voices, the Masked Boobies, the dolphins? Was everything a dream? Was Jesse Barnes going to wake me up in his usual gruff manner? Was I actually on a boat, or was that just another one of my fucked-up mind trips? Had I ever even been to Cairns? How much of my life was only in my mind and how much was actually real? Do I exist? If so, why? If not, how is that so?

Fuck!

It did my head in. I had so many questions and no answers at all. I sank fast into a whirlpool of despair. The dolphins must have morphed into Tiger Sharks and headed for the ocean floor, taking my hope with them.

Chapter Sixteen

'I'm on watch,

I'm on watch,

Drinking Scotch,

To stay on watch.'

The only way to fight off the Tiger Sharks was to beat them with a blunt instrument. Scotch was the apparatus of choice.

'God bless Barnes,' I thought, as I swigged at an expensive looking bottle of Chivas Regal.

Alcohol had always been my friend. Through all the years of love, drugs, hate, scorn, laughter, loneliness, senselessness, and hope, alcohol had been my constant and only companion. And there it was again, in my time of need.

The idea had been that it would work against the pills in my system, but I think I had taken things a little too far. Half a bottle had disappeared and I was starting to feel a little drowsy.

The Beche De Mer had turned into a tourist boat. We cruised around the mangroves, and a tour guide spoke to the crowd.

'So, pretty soon we should come across a basking female. They tend to sun themselves out in the open,' he said. 'But remember, they can jump over twice their body length, and can be extremely unpredictable.'

The bleach-blond tour guide suddenly put his finger to his lips as he spotted something towards the starboard (or is that port? I don't fucking know) side of the boat.

'Sssshhh. We don't want to get her angry.'

The flat-bottomed boat motored slowly towards the mud flat.

'There she is. Beautiful, isn't she?'

In the middle of the open space was Victoria, wearing nothing. Her skin was as brown as the mud surrounding her crossed legs. She lay flat on her back, her mouth wide open. Next to her was the mauled corpse of a dolphin, its milky eyes one of the few things left on its carcass.

'Now, she's just eaten and is still a bit drowsy. I think we can pull the boat in a little bit closer.'

Everyone in the crowd was on edge, myself included. I was wearing a red polo shirt and white shorts.

'This is neato,' I said to nobody in particular in an American accent. 'I mean, we get these in Florida too, but this is kinda cool. How about this heat?'

I was scared about getting too close to the wild animal, especially when Victoria became aware of our presence. Her head turned slowly towards us. Expressionless, her eyes glowed green.

She growled, grabbed the dolphin carcass in her mouth, and dragged it into the undergrowth. Feeling a bit more relaxed, the crowd sat down and started chatting. Out of the corner of my eye, I saw her figure slipping into the water and submerging.

I was considering telling the tour guide what I saw but my train of thought was interrupted by the boat capsizing.

Profanities were being screamed, as one-by-one their numbers were pulled under the water. Brown water turned into a weird orange, and finally, a glowing crimson.

'This isn't so neat,' I said to nobody in particular. I patiently awaited my turn, watching as the others disappeared around me. Victoria sprung up from the murk, two inches from my face.

'You have other things to attend to!' she hissed. 'Wake up and deal with what matters!'

Her face was mud-spattered. She had blood dripping from the corners of both sides of her mouth.

'Like, what the heck is that supposed to mean, you know?' I asked.

'Wake up! WAKE UP!'

Her last warning jolted me back to my seat in the wheelhouse. I'd been out for a while. The Beche De Mer was still travelling and there were no boats within sight. I saw Nathan and Stan both get out of the cabin at the same time. They were having an animated discussion, which developed into yelling, which I couldn't hear from behind the glass of the wheelhouse. Most probably the topic was not the relative influence of modern French sculpting and its use of negative space on modern architecture.

Yelling soon developed into violence. Not being particularly fond of either competitor, I didn't really care who won, although I disliked and envied Nathan a little bit more. One thing was for sure, there was no way I was going to intervene.

The guys looked like they'd deliberately placed themselves in front of the wheelhouse for my entertainment. I sat back in my corporate box and watched the action unfold.

The two competitors stood three metres apart, with their hands clenched, circling each other slowly. Nobody wanted to make the first move.

'Fucking get on with it!' I yelled at the glass.

Nathan and Stan were both shoeless and shirtless. They were wearing only shorts; Nathan had the tight, football variety. Stan was more formal with cargos. Even the roughest pub in Cairns would have refused them service.

Stan lunged towards Nathan and slipped over. Before he could get up off all fours, he was kicked in the stomach, sending him lying face first on the deck. Sensing his advantage, Nathan quickly laid in the foot a couple of times. Nathan thought, like I did, that it was over.

It wasn't.

With hindsight, Nathan may have changed his decision to leave Stan's crumpled mass alone for that split second. When he returned with the deck hose turned on, Stan was back up, and looking kind of pissed off. He slammed his fist straight into Nathan's chest. Even I heard the thud as Nathan doubled over, before receiving an uppercut to the face. The blows released the thick, heavy hose from Nathan's grasp and it started writhing around the deck, churning saltwater all over the place. Stan grabbed the hose and tried to whack Nathan baseball style, but the hose wasn't a great choice of weapon. It writhed and undulated with the pressure of the releasing sea water. Still, one hit from that weighty hose would put Nathan out of his self-obsessed brain. But Stan couldn't quite get a decent handle on it. With the hose wriggling, Nathan was ending up more wet than whacked.

Its ineffectiveness gave Nathan a chance to gather his composure and balance. Frustrated, Stan threw the rubber serpent away, letting it writhe freely.

If I had been a judge, I would have had both combatants on even points at that stage. They were both bleeding from various parts, with their blood thinning on the watery deck.

They were neck-and-neck and at each other's necks. The fighting got dirtier and sloppier, and soon the two were entangled on the floor. I couldn't tell if they were making love or war anymore. No, it was still war. Nathan had grabbed a fistful of Stan's sunkissed brown hair, and was smashing his face into the floor. Stan was wrenching Nathan's groin with his left hand and punching him with his right. I quietly took leave of my commentary box and crept out to where the action was.

With each head-smash to the floor, Stan was losing control and consciousness. I quietly turned the big fucker of a hose off and moved with it towards Nathan. He lifted Stan's head one final time and held it, pausing like a pro wrestler before he ends a fight. He couldn't resist the chance to say something tough before finishing him off.

'Make sure you say hello to....'

'The Captain,' I said, capping his quote. He looked up at me with anger and fear painting his dial.

Crack!

The deck hose connected to the front of Punt's turned head, rendering him limp and unconscious. He fell like a garbage-bag full of shit. The two warriors lay there side-by-side, like the gay lovers that, deep down, they had yearned to be.

The boys were no longer in a fighting mood so I headed back to the wheelhouse. Where was my scotch?

The boat was cruising pretty fast. I didn't know how to drive it and, since I'd loaded myself with Barnes' bounty, I wasn't likely to work it out any time soon. Looking to my right, water. Left, water. To my front and back? Nothing but salty H2O. I was a miniscule dot inside a miniscule boat, floating on the surface of a miniscule planet. Nobody cared about my miniscule situation.

I turned off the music. I thought I needed to think. I'd drunk all the scotch and was onto some of those pissy, light beers that we found in Barnes' room. That was typical fucking Jesse Barnes. All those threats of 'drinking you cunts under the table like the good old days,' and he's got a slab of lights stashed under his mattress. It was a good thing that he was dead. Still, the light beers certainly were good for clearing the head. 'Light beer. A drink to start the day with,' would have been a fitting marketing slogan.

Goliath and Goliath were still lying unconscious. They looked at peace. I had checked that they were both breathing; they were. That was as far as my understanding of first aid went. I was hoping that when they woke up, they would have amnesia. I'd tell them that their names were Sonny and Cher and that they were my personal servants.

'Sonny, you used to fluff my pillow thus!' I would say, with reserved patience.

'Cher, crouch down on all fours and be my coffee table. There's a good man-bitch.'

'Yes, you always wore pink dresses. They match those darling bonnets of yours so well.'

It suddenly occurred to me that if the Water Police pulled us over, I was as fucked as Elton John's arsehole on his second wedding night. On the upside, if I got busted, at least it would mean that I would have seen another living soul before I died. At the moment, that was looking unlikely. I was feeling as lonely and unfulfilled as Elton John's arsehole on his first wedding night.

That slight concern for my future meant that it was time to communicate with the only remaining conscious crew member on this fun-filled voyage: the much-silent Victoria.

I checked the satellite readings and other equipment as best as I could, forgot everything and went down to Victoria's room. Since Barnes had died, I hadn't seen her go to the toilet, to the shower, not at all. Fuck, she'd better be alive in there!

'Victoria,' I said, as I tapped gently on her door.

No response.

'Victoria.'

Nothing.

'Victoria. I need you to open the door. I need you to be alive. I need your help!'

Silence.

'Victoria! I am in a situation where I need you to help me. I know that you are upset. I know that you've lost a relative. I know that this situation must be hard for you. But you need to come out of your room right now. First, I don't know how to cook for myself, but slightly more pressing is the fact that Nathan and Stan are hurt, and Paul is all fucked up. I fucking don't know what to do, and I need help. I need help! I NEED HELP!'

I was crying as the door slowly opened, revealing the blonde, fragile girl that I was so fond of. Her blue eyes were wide open and bloodshot.

'Jesse Barnes is gone, but we still need to get back home safely. There is nothing we can do for him now,' I said in an undertaker's voice. 'And I am sorry for your loss,' I added, since I was in character.

All was silent. Time stopped.

'My loss? I just wish I'd killed the cunt myself.'

Missives Of Merpeople

Head Squihhsbah,

The target has done all of the work for me. He has overdosed on illicit human drugs and is drying to death as I imprint these messages to the sea. The captain of the craft, the one that I convinced to be my distant uncle, has drowned. This is cause for rejoice for both land and water dwellers. Two of the other crew are soon to perish due to civil violence. I may have to help the process along.

There is only one surviving crew member who knows of the target's 'Paul Hart' alias. This crew member, Kelvin Daniels, is neither reliable nor believable. When he is sober, which is rare, he is confused and generally seeking to be un-sober. I see no reason to kill him, rather I will keep him on observation in Holland with me until I am satisfied he has forgotten the one he knows as Paul Hart.

The Merhunter

Chapter Seventeen

I explained a few things to Victoria, mainly regarding the lack of conscious men around the place. She took my explanation of events pretty well, and without surprise.

Victoria explained a few things to me. First, she was well aware that Barnes' room was full of drugs. He ran the sea cucumber operation as a legitimate, highly profitable business, but it wasn't enough for a prick like Jesse Barnes. He made even more money by importing drugs into Australia and selling them to an unknown contact in Cairns.

She knew quite a bit for an innocent looking doll. This shipment of drugs was picked up only a few nights before. One night, very, very late, with Victoria's assistance, Barnes had quietly let the good dory drift away from the boat, with him on board. He waited until he was a safe distance away, fired up the engine and cruised to his rendezvous point. He came back unnoticed, and unloaded the bounty while all but Victoria slept.

Customs were 'taken care of,' to quote Barnes. Victoria was paid pretty handsomely to keep the rest of the crew (us) off the scent and to keep her eyes and ears out for anything suspicious. She was kept in the dark about almost everything else and that had been her duty for two years.

'There are more drugs in the engine room,' she said matter-of-factly.

Without being told directly, Victoria knew she was in big, violent trouble if she ever spoke a word to anybody. I was the first person she'd ever told.

Barnes, I had thought previously, was a miserable, angry, fat prick. From what Victoria was telling me, those were by far his good qualities. The man was a hardened criminal.

'What would he say if anybody asked him about suspicious noises?' I asked.

'You know him. "You're more fucking useless than I thought!' He'd just squawk abuse until they forgot about it. That's probably why he was so aggressive to everyone he worked with from the outset. It didn't seem out of character when he went off at people like that.'

'That and the fact that he was a peerless arsehole.'

'Precisely. There was one guy that wouldn't let up about it though. What was his name? Frank, I think. The whole trip he kept asking about the noises he heard on the third night. He was probably hoping for some shut-the-fuck-up money. Anyway, once back on land, I think Uncle Jesse convinced him to be quiet without having to part with any cash. I saw him about a month later with bandages around his head. He ran away from me.'

'So what do we do now?'

'Well, Kelvin, for starters, you can go back on watch. You will drown and die if we crash into another boat.'

'What do I do if I actually see anything?'

'Use the steering wheel to go around it.'

'Okay, I'll get back into the wheelhouse. What are you going to do?'

'I'm going to think of a way to get your sorry head out of this situation.'

After watching a fight, knocking out Nathan, and discovering this new, street-wise Victoria, I was back to wearing my cheapo sunglasses and staring out at nothing. According to the map on the computer, we still had a long long way to go. What we were going to do when we got back on shore was another issue entirely.

The blue carpet expanded to all corners. Ever since Robert Palmer had spoken to me, my seasickness had stopped. Maybe it was the drugs. Drugs! I'd nearly forgotten about those things. I quickly washed down a mystery pill with some beer, then ate some marijuana; I figured it would be irresponsible to smoke it inside. Barnes seemed to have tried to diversify in the drug market. Good thing, that.

After a while, the blue sea and the blue sky had completely blued out my world. I was tired and wired by the time Victoria appeared beside me.

'All right, I've got a plan.'

'Huh. What is it?'

She looked deep into my eyes and then surveyed the rest of my body.

'Have you been taking any more drugs?'

'Not excessively, just some groovy pills and whatnot. Why do you ask?'

'Part one of the plan is that, if you touch any other substances in here, I'm going to throw you overboard myself. This is fucking serious. In twelve hours you are going to be back in Cairns, and in big trouble,' she said, and then paused. 'Are you with me, Kelvin?'

'No worries, thanks, I'll look into it,' I mumbled, as I crawled underneath the desk and shut my eyes.

'That answer doesn't make sense. You are a fucking useless waster!'

'You are a fucking useless waster!' I mimicked in a high-pitched, stupid voice.

'For fuck's sake, I don't sound like that.'

'Mor mucks make, blah bleh bla bla bla.'

I laughed myself to sleep.

And again I was dreaming, but it was dreaming with a purpose. I had control of my dream world. I envisaged myself driving the Beche-de-mer. In my dream land, I knew how to control the boat. I was wearing a white captain's uniform, straight out of The Love Boat. There was no wave action at all. The sun was out and not too bright, but I still felt justified in wearing my aviator sunglasses. So did my co-pilot. Robert Palmer sat next to me in similar attire, except he was smoking.

'You know, those things must have helped in killing you,' I said, pointing at his cigarette.

'So, why should I quit now?' he replied in his masculine British accent.

'Fair point, mate.'

'Kelvin, you are in some seriously heavy nova. Tell me, what options have you explored to get you out of this situation?'

'Well, I thought that we could bring the boat back to Cairns and take it from there.'

'A boat full of drugs, minus the captain, with three corpses on board?'

'There are no corpses on board, Mr Palmer. I believe that you are the only corpse aboard the Beche De Mer.'

'They're not dead?'

'No.'

'Well, they must be pretty close, I was just talking to.... Look, that's not the point. The point is, that driving back to Cairns with all of this illegal shit going on is the stupidest idea I've heard since my producer suggested I have a cartoon backing-band for the "Change his Ways" music video.'

'Oh, the yodelling song?'

'Yes. Nobody ever calls it by its name, even in the afterlife.'

'Those were the hottest cartoon ducks ever. Did you shag one?'

'Is that rhetorical?'

'Was that rhetorical?'

'Kelvin, enough of this. You are wasting my allotted vision time. Do you have a plan?'

'I guess we throw the drugs overboard and then we cruise back to Cairns. We run the boat into the mangroves, give our apologies to the crocodiles, and have a nice steak at the Hog's Breath Café.'

'Drugs float, bodies float. They'll turn up.'

'There are no bodies. What bodies?'

'Barnes probably has drugs stashed all over the boat. It might be impossible to find them all. The police will search the whole thing, inside and out. They will check every carpet fibre, tile, blood stain, skid mark, cum splurge and toenail picking in the place. It won't look good for you. They are also going to wonder what happened to your crew. The Beche De Mer is a life sentence in waiting. Kelvin, are you listening?'

'Yeah, I'm with you. I was just wondering who the most famous bird you ever rooted is?'

'It is a tie between Annie Lennox and Grace Jones. That was one wild night, I can tell you.'

'I'm impressed, Bobby-boy!'

'As were they. But that's not the point, and you are not to address me by that alias,' he said firmly but politely.

'Sorry, Mr. Palmer.'

'What I'm getting at, is that the last place this boat should end up is Cairns, or any other port for that matter.' He drew on his never-ending cigarette. 'The Beche De Mer belongs with Barnes.'

'You mean, we should chop it up and feed it to sharks and turtles?'

'The boat, the bodies, and the drugs belong with Barnes.'

'Look, Mr Palmer, I'm going to start ignoring you if you keep referring to my crew as bodies. They are alive!'

'Are they?'

'Alive, Alive, ALIVE!'

We both stared at each other. He had a look of stern defiance on his face, which he kept until he spoke.

'Kelvin, I've taken you far enough. I can't tell you anymore. You know the rules. I can only talk in frustratingly mysterious tones. So, what you do now is up to you. I have faith in you. The heat is on, but you can get through it. Now I must go.'

'Until the next time you appear.'

'That's right.'

'In five minutes.'

'Not if you keep giving me this attitude.'

'Okay. So, crazy man, it all belongs with Barnes. Is that your final word on things?'

'I'm saner than you. I don't have Kelvin Daniels visiting me in my dreams.'

The man was more than just class. He was just as at home in a slanging match as he was in his private limousine.

'Nice one,' I conceded. 'Just one last question, or a clarification really.'

'Go ahead, my most testing friend.'

'In your song 'Bad Case of Loving You,' who is you? Cos the line goes: "Doctor doctor, give me the news, I've got a bad case of loving you." Is the doctor in love with you, or are you in love with the doctor? Or, is you a separate person that the doctor has diagnosed the first person as loving?'

'The answer to that is simple. Trust in yourself. Don't call me Palmy, and believe.'

'How does the boat belong with Barnes?'

'You'll see very soon.'

And again, he vanished. I woke up. Even my delusional creations were crazy; what hope did I have?

I ran to the back deck and found Victoria.

'What should we do?' I yelled over the roar of the wind.

'Sink the boat.'

'Did Robert Palmer intimate that to you too?'

'No he didn't,' she said, sighing.

'What on earth am I going to do with you in Amsterdam?' she muttered, as she disappeared indoors.

My spirits uplifted, I laughed at the ocean for a while. When I returned, I found Victoria scribbling in her green notebook. It read in her beautifully feminine handwriting:

JESSE BARNES—DEAD OVERBOARD

NATHAN PUNT—DEAD ON BOARD

PAUL HART—DEAD ON BOARD

STAN DWYER—DEAD ON BOARD

KELVIN DANIELS—ALIVE

VICTORIA BARNES—ALIVE

'You seem to have made a misjudgement with Messrs Punt, Hart, and Dwyer,' I said, as I scanned the list. 'Don't you mean "unconscious"?'

'Well, they are "unconscious" for all time now. They've checked out, stopped breathing. They are dead. It was very respectful of you to build a castle of crap over Paul Hart. I'm sure he's beaming down at you from heaven.'

'But he was breathing not too long ago.'

'Look, I'm sorry too, Kelvin. I checked on them and none of them had a pulse. We should probably have dragged them onto their sides or something.'

Heavy nova. That was the last time I'd try to correct Robert Palmer.

'How do we sink this boat?'

'I figured that if we use the deck hose to fill up all of the air spaces below deck with sea water, we can make this ship go down. We can use one of the dories either to get to land or to find a ship and raise the alarm.'

'All right. So we want to sink the boat while we are still in really deep water, yeah? Are we in deep water?'

'Yes we are, Kelvin. I sense we are about 1.7 kilometres above the ocean floor right now. If this boat goes down in that sort of water, it will be impossible to trace and recover. But we want to be close enough to the mainland that we don't get lost and die out here, like the others have.'

'Are you sure they're dead?'

'Look Kelvin, I checked them and they are fucking dead. Now fucking listen to me or you'll join them,' she cursed, showing for the first time that she is a Barnes.

'I'll be silent and listen,' I said submissively.

'According to the autopilot we've got nineteen hours until we get back within the Great Barrier Reef. We want to be absolutely certain that this thing is sunk by then. With Dwyer gone, there's nobody here who knows how to shut off the engine or turn this thing around. I've tried for ages, but this thing will not stop heading towards Cairns.'

'I'll start filling it up now.'

So, without hesitation, I did what I was told. It was a pretty sunny day, and mid-afternoon by the look of things. I made sure not to step on Punt or Dwyer, who were still lying on their backs on the deck.

'Having a nice sunbake?' I asked, callously. Cabin fever can really turn you into a heartless prick.

I grabbed the deck hose and jammed the business end of it between the door and the door frame of the cabin. I turned the hose on full bore and started operation Sink fucking Beche De Mer.

All of the pornography, filthy clothes and general man-waste of my former home were getting drenched in the substance it had protected me from for weeks and weeks. I didn't know whether to feel good or bad at the thought. It was best not to think too much. There was not too much for me to do, except plead with Victoria to give me back my stash.

I found her standing on the top deck, staring out into the all-encompassing blueness. Her blonde hair was waving in the breeze, as if from a Whitesnake film clip. As always, she looked calm and in control.

Noticing me, she looked at me with her not-even-a-fucking-chance-in-hell-you're-going-to-get-anything-out-of-me-you-useless-dependent-waster eyes. Acting on that, I tried to make as if I was there for another reason.

'What should we do with these bodies?' I asked.

'What do you think?'

'We could eat them.'

'I guess, or we could make some nice lamp-shades out of their skin.'

'We could make full body puppets out of them. You can wear a Stan suit and I'll wear a Nathan suit. We could put on a children's show.'

'Good idea. We can have a section of the show on how we made them and how we used the rest of their bodies for the sausage rolls everybody is eating.'

'Hmmm,' I said, and paused for a long while.

'Jesus Christ, you're not actually thinking about that, are you?' she asked.

'No, no, no. Sorry. Leave it with me. I'll take care of it.'

'Just put them somewhere out of the way, please,' were her parting instructions.

Wanting to impress Victoria, and to use the mysterious advice offered by Robert Palmer, I decided it was time to dispose of the bodies.

So, first, I dragged the former Mr Hart's body out onto the front deck, lining him up next to the other two guys. Passing into death hadn't really changed Paul Hart's personality. I quickly rifled through their pockets to see if they had any stuff. I collected two half-filled pouches of tobacco, some dope, a lighter, a photo of a hot woman and a condom produced by a company that folded in the '90s. I realised then that I should have gone through all of their stuff in the cabin before turning the hose on it. Oh well, I'd remember that for next time.

Those guys really were dead. They hadn't been that dead before I passed out. Was that unusual? I dunno, I'm not a doctor. What I did know was that they were already getting baked in the sun and I wanted rid of them. More importantly, Victoria had left it up to me to deal with them. It was my chance to impress her. Think, Kelvin, think.

Weight belts!

We had a whole stack of them on the back deck, right outside the toilet. They were no use to anyone who was alive, except for the use I was about to put them to. I dragged Hart by the legs out to the back deck via the thin strip of deck on the port (I think) side. His head kept bumping into stuff and he was leaving a trail of strangely coloured blood. Once I had him close to the back railing, I strapped two, heavy weight belts around his waist. He smelt of sea cucumbers. With all my strength, I managed to hurl his body up onto the back railing. His head and torso hung over the side, looking out to sea. I grabbed his legs and flipped him overboard. He did one-and-a-half somersaults and hit the water. He had over-rotated dreadfully and did not achieve the bubble entry I was hoping for. The judges wouldn't have liked that. He disappeared the moment he hit the water's surface. He was where he always excelled and truly belonged. As a sign of respect, I bowed my head and said a few words about the man I knew nothing about.

'Paul Hart, I know you are at peace in the realm where you belong. Take care, and try not to catch too many sea cucumbers while you are down there. Oh, and lay off the drugs, mate.'

As for Nathan and Stan, I didn't really care. They killed each other on my watch, which was out of order. I dumped them over one by one, although, physically, it was a lot harder with those two oafs than it was with the Hart-man.

'Get fucked, Nathan.'

'So long, Stan, ay?'

As they sank out of existence, I started yelling the Australian national anthem, using swear words for the many parts I didn't know.

'By golly! How disrespectful of your country and of the deceased.'

The Masked Booby had returned. It was his voice, but I couldn't see him anywhere.

'Where are you?' I asked.

'I have a vantage point where I can see you and that is all that should concern you, old chum.'

'I'm not your chum, and I'm not that old. Fuck off!' I yelled to the sky.

'I'm dreadfully sorry; I am merely here to assist. I'm not that fond of you either. But never mind, I will help you out. You remind me of the young man I once was.'

'What the fuck? I can think of a few differences. Like the fact that I grew up in Melbourne with a pair of hands and a distinct lack of feathers.'

'I grew up in Melbourne, you know.'

'Fuck off. I've already got Robert Palmer here to help me out.'

'That washed-up old rock star is nothing but a spectacular nuisance. Would you listen to someone who still smokes cigarettes and drinks malt whiskey, even though it killed him? Or would you listen to—'

'Someone that shits where he eats,' I cut in.

'That is a greater talent to have than you will ever know,' he said earnestly. 'I also shit *while* I eat.

'Now why on Earth did you just dump the bodies of your colleagues into the Coral Sea?' His voice had become more sinister and authoritative.

'Because they were dead.'

'And why did they die?'

'They were fucked up and—' It was the bird's time to cut in on me.

'Breathing!' he yelled. 'Those young lads were breathing the last time you saw them!'

'What are you saying, mate?'

'Young chap, what I am implying is quite simple. That young mistress may not be as helpless and innocent as you think.'

'Where are you?'

I still could not see any white 'm-shapes' anywhere on the horizon. It was getting to be too much.

'She knew all about the drugs on-board the boat. She disappeared when your captain came back half-dead. She discovered that the rest of the crew had died. Do you not find that at all suspicious?'

'I hadn't. I've been a bit wasted, though.'

'And whose fault is that?'

'Mine, not Victoria's. She keeps hounding me about my substance abuse. She calls me a waster all the time. She's good. She likes me. She wants the best for me. She wants to travel with me to Amsterdam.'

'My poor, misguided lad. I fear that you are in grave peril. Victoria is a harsh and cold state, as is the woman.'

'No, she's not.' I yelled into the sky.

'You're not quite listening to my expert opinion. Although Mr Palmer means well, he is but a foolish motivational speaker.'

'No, he is not. He is the only—'

'Stop being so blazing defensive. This, my boy, is going to hurt me much more than it will hurt you.'

I stared out at the ocean, while the intense pressure inside my mind threatened to explode.

RAAARRRKKKKK!

Out of nowhere, I was set upon by Sir Masked Booby and his cronies. They zoomed out of nowhere and pecked at my legs, torso, and neck. They pulled all of my body hair and, fuck, did they squawk up a storm.

'Yes, yes, my stupid lad. You had to learn this the hard way. Don't trust anyone. Not Victoria, not Robert Palmer, not me, not even yourself. RAAAARRRKKK!'

His last primal tweet seemed to be an order for his crew to stop butchering me. In an instant, they were flying off towards the horizon, leaving me on the ground with their leader perched on my chest. Somehow, he was as heavy as an anvil; I could barely breathe.

'Ask what's going on, and see what her reaction is, young boy.'

Chapter Eighteen

After recovering from the attack, I went up to the wheelhouse, where Victoria was looking out towards the horizon.

'Are you all right?' she asked.

'Yeah, why?'

'I could hear some birds squawking back there. They weren't picking at the bodies, were they?'

'No,' I said, trying to move on.

'Great,' she said.

'Hey Victoria,' I said.

'Yes, stupid, yet somehow likeable waster,' she replied.

Pausing for a stunned, flattered second, I finally asked, 'You didn't happen to kill everyone that was on this boat except for me, did you?'

She looked back at me, stunned.

'No Kelvin, I didn't. However, if I had, do you think that asking me like that would have been the best course of action?'

'No. It's— Well,' I mumbled into my chin, 'well, the guys were still breathing and stuff, and then the birds thought...'

'Look, Kelvin!' she instructed, snapping me out of my adolescent stupor. 'We are in a pretty dire situation. You and I need to work together as a team. I did not kill anybody and do not intend to. Without you, I can't get out of this. I want us to help each other.

'Kelvin!' She said loudly, demanding my attention. 'Look at me.'

I looked at her. She was a frustrated beauty.

'You have average looks. You have a penchant for mind-altering substances. You are apathetic, verging on completely pathetic.

'You haven't learnt a thing from life. You ignore life. You treat life like it is an obstacle in between you and the beer fridge.'

'Thanks for the pep talk,' I zinged.

'It is a pep talk; an honest pep talk,' she replied.

She paused and looked at her hands as if trying to find an answer.

'This is difficult to explain, but I'll try to.'

She looked at me with genuine emotion before talking again.

'I know you, Kelvin. I can sense who you really are. When you are under the water, you radiate aliveness. You take everything in. You are in the moment. You take command. You make decisions and stick by them. You don't drift with the tide when you are under the water, but you do above the waves.

'I like you, Kelvin. I can tell that you are a good man; a good person. I don't want you to change. You are occasionally funny above the water, and a beauty underneath. That is why I want to travel with you after we sort this mess out.

'But first, Kelvin, I want you to make love to me.'

She slipped off her brown cords, revealing her tanned legs and pink panties.

'Let's fuck.'

I only really honed in on the last two words that she had said and started mauling her neck and unbuttoning her shirt. My left hand slid underneath her knickers, and I felt around for her clitoris—fucking stupid things. But I could feel her getting wetter and heard her moans getting louder. I ripped her underwear off her and got down onto my knees.

Unusually, I took some of the many words of advice that Nathan Punt had given me during our time together.

'If you can make her orgasm before she even sees your cock, then you can do whatever the fuck you want with the bitch after.'

So, I growled away at her pussy as if I was a bloodhound and she was on her rags. I didn't really know what I was doing, but I could tell from the way she was clawing at my head that I was doing something very right. It tasted like I imagined sea cucumbers would.

'Fucking Yes! YES! YES!' she screamed, so loud that people in Cairns could hear her.

She rammed her pussy onto my nose and mouth. My head was jammed up somewhere around her lower intestine. My hands were all over her and I could feel her stomach tensing. I was sure that if I stopped, she would kill me.

'YEEESSSSS!'

She went limp on the kitchen table. I stood back and admired my work for a second. Fuck, she was beautiful. Her hair was wild and frizzed, her tits perky, despite the fact that she was flat on her back. Her panting made her flat belly rise and fall. Her legs were still apart and her blond pussy looked inviting.

'And now, I get to do whatever the fuck I like,' I thought, as I took off my shorts and rested both of her feet up on my shoulders.

Fucking hell. That was fucking magic.

After a legend's session all over the place, checking occasionally that the boat wasn't about to crash, we rested in the captain's bed. I was feeling like the admiral of the HMAS Universe. This trip was going to work out just fine. Me and Victoria, Victoria and me. Heading to Europe together. I pictured the story:

As the Beche De Mer is just about to sink, we head into Barnes favourite dory and cruise to the coastline. We get our stories straight and then we find the nearest town. The cops ask us a few questions, see there is nothing suspicious, and we get in the local newspaper as a feel-good story of survival. We then go to Europe and get married in Luxembourg, have four daughters, and run our own chain of waffle houses all over the world. When it is time for us to retire, we divide the business into four quarters to give to our four daughters, who all sell up straight away and become 'famous socialites' (i.e. rich sluts). Candice, the youngest, releases a pop single, 'Giving Hope fo Shizzle,' which sucks beyond belief. We then move on to ridding the world of war and weapons, which we think we have completed, until we get shot at ages sixty-one and sixty-two, respectively.

When we both woke after the briefest of naps, I thought I might engage in a bit of pillow talk.

'So, if I hadn't already dumped those other three in the ocean, I bet they would have wanted to make this a five-way, or even a six way if Barnes was still around. Not that I'm hugely into group necrophilia, or cock.'

My mutterings of sweet nothings made Victoria sit bolt upright.

'What did you say?'

'About cock?'

'Kelvin. Did you throw Paul Hart overboard?'

'Yes I did, along with the other two. I used my own initiative based on supernatural advice.'

'Right. Now let me get this clear. You didn't dream this. He, sorry, the three of them, have been turfed?'

'Yes. Umm, do you want to have sex again?'

'I really do but I can't. I have to go. Kelvin, please don't take this as a sign of my not liking you. I meant what I said about Amsterdam: you are the only human I have wanted to spend time with. I sincerely hope I get to see you again, but for now, I am going to have to jump overboard.'

Victoria then raced, naked, out of the Captain's quarters and up the stairs. I pounded after her in time to see her perfect arse disappearing into the water off the back deck.

The boat kept rolling on, getting slowly lower in the water. I was still basking in post-shag afterglow and then suddenly had to deal with the fact that Victoria seemed to commit suicide shortly after I had blown all over her tits. Luckily I had an ideal coping mechanism for all of that, so I grabbed a bottle of spirits and smoked up a few spliffs until I stopped worrying. I sat in the wheelhouse, not worrying for a while, until the boat jolted with a huge cracking sound and stopped completely. It was dark, so I went to sleep.

Missives Of Merpeople

Head Squihhsbah,

Circumstances have changed. Kelvin has thrown the target's body overboard, thus unintentionally saving his life. I am in pursuit of the target right now.

The Merhunter

Head Squihhsbah,

I have failed. I am slain. I am retreating to the depths in the slim hope of recovery. The target is still free.

The Merhunter

Chapter Nineteen

I woke at dawn. I was scared, confused, heartbroken and bored. The boat was stationary and firmly embedded in a beautiful looking coral reef.

'Why not go for a dive?' I asked myself, looking out towards the rising sun and the water.

It wasn't too difficult to assemble the required gear. Before the Beche De Mer had turned into a boat of death, it was a boat of diving. Most of the cylinders, wetsuits, and assorted pieces of equipment were still intact on the back deck. I had to do my own buddy-check before I dropped off the back of the boat and once again entered the world that doesn't shun me.

Shoals of tiny, bluey-greeny fish were swimming in tight gangs. Their cousins, the tiny white and black striped fish, hid among the coral. There were turtles, stingrays, and moray eels out. Warren had told me that the early morning was the best time to dive. He said that all the night animals were still partying, while the morning animals were just getting up. It was similar to a Sunday morning in central Melbourne, when those unfortunate enough to be going to work are greeted by those who are still on a night out.

Everything swam with me that morning. A remora attached itself to me, reef sharks cruised by and catfish foraged. The world was temporarily submerged and at peace. A cease-fire had been declared, the umpire had called time out. For that moment, everything belonged to each other, and I was included. The aggression of the sea was absent, not just on my reef, but in the whole ocean. I could feel it through the water. Miles from the reef, great white sharks were swimming happily through pods of obliging dolphins. Fishermen were kissing their catch, apologising and releasing their surprised bounty back into the pool of life and love. Whales and submarines danced the dosey-doe in the ocean depths, all because of the love emanating from the reef. Victoria was out there somewhere, thinking of me.

Kelvin's reef. Kelvin's ocean. Kelvin's heaven.

A big, pristine Wally swam towards me. He was much bigger than me and gleamed with green health. As he swam past me, with minimal movement, he showed off the many beautiful patterns on the side of his body, and before he jetted off, he winked.

For the first and last time of my life, I belonged.

I didn't want to go back to the Beche De Mer. I felt the pull of the ocean, and I responded. I started heading down deeper and deeper, away from the pretty corals and sunshine. It was getting darker; the sun's rays were fading as fast as my resolution to ever return to the surface. I kept descending deeper, closer to the earth's core. The coral went grey; the fish, absent. The deeper I went, the closer to home I knew I was. This was my family. This was where I was supposed to be.

I checked my computer—it said something like sixty metres deep. I don't really remember; I didn't really care.

'You're a daft twat, innit?'

Neville walked towards me.

'Why do you say that, Ginger-balls?' I asked the casually dressed Neville.

'You should've come with me, innit? If you'd followed me, you'd be in the outback, under the stars, banging lassies like I've been doin' every feckin' night, innit?'

Although he was an apparition, I could still tell when he was lying.

'You couldn't pick up flies off dog shit, mate.'

'Well, guv, the only thing you'll be picking up is AIDS from the many anal rapings you'll be getting' in the clink, innit? That is assuming you don't drown.'

He had a point.

'Well, what do I do?'

'I don't know, guv.'

'Well, fuck off then!'

'Don't get your Bristols in a twist. Fine, I'll fuck off then, back to the lassies, if ya know what I mean, eh, eh?!'

He walked away, waving his arms as if pretending to swim. I missed him.

Then it was my parents' turn. They pulled up in their Ford Falcon.

'Kelvin,' said Mum, 'you should be eating better. And maybe a phone call every now and then wouldn't go astray.'

'We're not surprised, son,' said Dad. 'We've just about had enough of this.'

Then they drove off.

It was dark all around me. No colours, no fish, no hope. The world above me had nothing left to offer.

'YOU FUCKING CUNT!' squawked Barnes, as he flapped his arms in the air. 'YOU FUCKING BENT ME, DROWNED ME, FED ME TO THE SHARKS AND FUCKED MY NIECE!'

'YEAH, SIMULTANEOUSLY!' I mimicked back at him, flapping my arms in a parody of the ex-Captain. 'I didn't kill you, but I was certainly thinking about it when I was fucking your relative.

'By the way, Skipper, you're looking a lot better than when I last saw you. You seem to be, you know, not distributed between several sharks.'

That was the bravest I'd ever been with him. Maybe it's because he was dead, or was I dead? Hmmm.

'YOU WERE A FUCKING USELESS CATCHER, KELVIN! FUCKING USELESS!'

'Well, you were a useless captain and nobody will miss you.'

'YOU NEITHER!'

'Fuck off.'

'DON'T YOU TELL ME TO FUCK OFF. I'LL FUCKING KILL YOU, YOU FUCKING CUUUUUUUNNNNNNNT!'

And then he merged into the water around him, his final word to me still echoing through the ocean.

'You've always been a smart cunt, ay?'

'Don't call him smart. He's not smart at all.'

'Are you a being a smart cunt, ay?'

'What the fuck do you think? Of course I'm being smart. I'm smarter than you.'

'Right. I'll fucking have to kill you again, ay?'

'It wasn't you. It was that tool over there.'

Nathan and Stan both looked at me

'Come on, Nathan,' I said in a calming tone of voice. 'I was acting in self-defence on Stan's behalf.'

'Youse always talked like a poof, ay?'

'All I know is that me and Stan are dead, and you're not! You killed us! You killed Hart, and Barnes! You killed Victoria! We're all dead because of you!'

'Yeah, ay?'

I took a moment to reflect on that accusation—and an accusation was all that it was, right? Ay? I really hoped so. Was I that crazy that I could have killed a whole crew of people and not realised it? Surely not. I flicked through my memory files but found them too obscured with drugs, alcohol and nitrogen to trust myself. But why was I alive by myself on the boat? Was I a victim of circumstance or was I the cause of the circumstances and the killer of victims. Did Victoria really jump? Who does that? What the fuck was going on?

Nathan and Stan had disappeared back to hell, belting the shit out of each other all the way down.

'Did you kill me too?' asked a white and cold Victoria.

'Surely I couldn't do that. I don't know, I DON'T KNOW ANYMORE!' I bellowed out in a primal scream of tears and sadness.

Then Paul Hart swam past. His thin frame burst through the disappearing, ghostly vision of Victoria. He stopped to take an unemotional look and proceeded into the ether.

They were replaced by two familiar figures that I had never seen together before.

'Why, of course you are capable of murder. If you're barmy enough to accept that a bird is talking to you in excess of fifty metres underwater, then of course you are capable, young man. Extremely capable. RAARRRKKKK!'

'Don't be put off by him, or anyone else. They're not real, Kelvin. I'm the only one who's real.'

'Thanks, Mr. Palmer. I see you've got a silver suit on today. Looking good.'

'Of course I'm looking good. I am Robert Palmer.'

'Yeah, and you can smoke underwater. You make smoking look so cool.'

'As just discussed, I am Robert Palmer, and everything I do is cool. But our feather-preening friend and I have got more pressing matters than my image. My image isn't ever an issue, because I am perfect.'

'Robert, although it is most unusual for me to do so, I am inclined to agree with you on this occasion, with the exception of your accusation of me being a falsity. I am more real than you. You are a dead has-been' said the bird, before continuing.

'And I tell the boy how it is! You continue to give him clues, hints and omens. Look at the lad! He doesn't understand a blooming thing at the best of times.'

'I am Robert Palmer and I am too in control to argue with sea fowl. We need to save him.'

'Correct, Robert. We must talk to the young chap.'

They stopped their bickering and turned their attention to me.

'Kelvin my boy, you are in trouble,' said the Masked Booby.

'That's true, Kelvin. You're descending deeper and deeper into the depths of your mind and the ocean, which is dangerous,' added Palmy.

'I don't want to leave the ocean. I belong here. I want to die here.'

'RAAARRRRKKK! The frightful thing is if you die, then we die. And, that just won't do, now, will it? So, hurry along back up to the surface like a good little Australian.'

'But, I belong down here, not up there. I'll be in trouble up there, lots of trouble.'

'Young Kelvin, I would suggest that the afterlife could be made into quite a miserable phase of eternity for you, if you don't do as we wish,' suggested the bird.

'Are you threatening me?'

'Don't worry about him; he's rarking mad. I've got some advice for you, son.'

'Are you my father, Mr Palmer?'

'God, no. I meant that as a term of endearment. I'm a celebrity. I wouldn't father a person like you. But I will give you some very important, but still cryptic, advice — through song.'

And then, Robert Palmer produced a microphone. A bevy of beauties in tight, mini dresses appeared behind him. Some of them formed an eight-piece band that started an eighties groove. Some of them danced. Many did nothing but look slicked back, tight, and hot. Palmy's gravelly voice assaulted the microphone.

There ain't nothing great about the great unknown,

We all get there someday, so just leave it alone,

If you ain't too happy being who you are,

Just give it some time and you might be a star.

The brass section wailed.

He jived behind his microphone as the band hit its strides. A wailing keytar solo by a hot chick was matched by a wailing double-guitar solo by a similarly hot chick. When Robert Palmer approached his microphone, I could tell it was time for the chorus.

'Ordinary people do amazing things,

Even emus sometimes get to flap their wings,

Gotta buy the ticket to go on that tram,

Gotta love yourself to be a better man.'

The band ripped into an instrumental break, while Robert Palmer danced like the tipsy accountant at the office Christmas party. The Masked Booby was joined at another microphone by four of the hot chicks and the rest of his bird crew. They beamed to the thumping '80s rock in a surprisingly beautiful harmony.

'This vocal line, is slightly more blunt,

Don't kill yourself, you fucking dumb cunt,

This vocal line, is slightly more blunt,

Don't kill yourself, you fucking dumb cunt.'

Then the band stopped dead, save the sexy drummer, who kept pounding out a thudding beat.

Robert Palmer punched his vocals over the hammer of the snare drum:

'SO, BUDDY YOU ARE LOOKING AT A FORK IN THE ROAD,

WITH YOUR 'XISTENCE, LUNGS, MIND, HEART, AND SOUL ALL SET TO EXPLODE,

YOU CAN DIE RIGHT HERE, RIGHT NOW, AMONG THE CORAL AND FISH,

OR YOU CAN KEEP US ALL ALI-YIVE!

BE TRUE TO YOUR WISH!'

And the band thundered back in, as the back-up singers moved and sang to the rhythm:

'Just so we are clear on what's being said,

Get out of the water, we don't want you dead.

Just so we are clear on what's being said,

Get out of the water, we don't want you dead.

The back-up harem/flock kept repeating the last two lines as the song gradually faded out. The band, the birds and the man fell farther and farther beneath me as I rose towards the surface, as if by magic. I wasn't swimming, but I wasn't struggling against the magical upward momentum. I accepted my reality and went with it.

Chapter Twenty

Fuck! What happened? I had been patiently waiting to drown to the funky stylings of Robert Palmer, and then... Who knows? There were a few questions running around my soaked noggin:

How was I back on this fucking-fuck-fuck-fucker of a boat?

Why was I lying half naked on the front deck?

I jumped up, with some discomfort, and ran to the port-side railing to check if the ocean was still there. It was; it was just like I left it. I didn't have time to feel relieved as I had slammed my cock hard into the metal of the banister in my eagerness. As I lay back down with my hands over my groin somebody placed a blanket over me.

Chapter Twenty-one

There was still no sign of my blanket provider, so I lay down on the cold blue fibreglass of the back deck. I was mentally tired, or retarded (I wasn't sure which) and physically rooted. With a million thoughts a second going through my mind—predominantly involving dead people, seabirds, pornography and beer—I instructed my brain:

'Settle down there, mate. I have actually got some thinking to do. Give me a couple of minutes of proper clarity and then we can both go downstairs and I'll jack off to whoever you think worthy.'

If the Coral Coppers had turned up at the Beche De Mer right then I would have been queried about murder, possession of a shit-load of drugs, damaging a heritage-listed natural wonder of the world, grand theft marine, driving a commercial sea vehicle without a licence whilst completely toasted and soliciting advice from unrecognised religious beings.

It seemed like it was time for some proper action.

'Okay, think, Kelvin, think. You need to get the fuck out of here, now, and not with the help of the Masked Booby or any eighties rock stars. This time, it is just you. So how do we get back home and off this thing?'

Spurred into action, I fell into an oxygen-filled slumber, leaving my mind to do its business, while my body rested.

When I woke up, I knew exactly what to do.

'Thanks, brain, I owe you one,' I said out loud as I woke up, more than a little bit cold.

'Who were you saying that to?'

'Myself. Who's asking?'

'My name is Jendaya.'

She was real, I was pretty sure.

'Did you save my life?'

'Yes.'

'Cheers.'

The Jendaya Chronicle: Part Five

I was able to edge my way out of South Africa by murdering and robbing the men who always picked me up in their cars. Some of the men tried to talk me out of doing something silly, and some of them tried to take the gun from me. Those were short trips in the car for me and an even more shortened life for them.

My assets expanded over this period. If it looked like I was not going to be able to kill my assailant, I was instead able to bribe my way out of trouble. Soon I was able to bribe and kill my way through the bent and corrupt lands of the Congo and Ethiopia. Occasionally, I resorted to buying a legitimate ticket for a bus or a train, but mostly I would spill blood to get to my next destination. Sometimes I pretended to be a prostitute in order to disarm, rob and kill men. I don't recall killing any women, but there were so many killings, it is hard to be sure. The more I travelled, the more I could recognise the types of men I wanted to kill. Men who dealt in illegal things, such as drugs and girls, tended to walk the streets in a very similar way. It was not hard to gain their interest. All I would have to do is walk near them and they would immediately come to see who I belonged to. I showed no mercy when the time came to end them. It never brought my family back, but every kill made me feel closer to them somehow.

I feared that I would soon become known for my actions within Africa, so when I had a chance to buy a ticket to India on an illegal boat, I took it. I didn't even have to kill anyone to acquire it.

Our craft was leaky and full of other desperate people. We were all worried that our horrible craft was going to sink at any time. In such an instance, my weapons, money and increasing bloodlust would have done me no good. I was restless and ready to channel my rage when I disembarked in India. The people-smugglers who aided my transport were the first ones to be relieved of their money and their lives. From there, the old pattern took over, although with the huge crowds in India I was rarely picked up in a car. There was a surprising amount of money around the slums and shanty towns and I was becoming very good at my trade. I was no longer opportunistic or passive. I knew where to find trouble and how to make it my kind of trouble.

Initially, my killing was an outlet for grief and rage and revenge. But when I was in India, it was a means to an end. I had nothing against the people of India. Most of my victims were very courteous and even generous. None were spared.

The American dollars that were worth the world in Africa were not so useful in India, so, instead, blood-stained rupees filled my stolen bags. I knew that my time was running out, that my name would soon become infamous and I should try to move on.

I never thought that I would end up so close to Australia. In my previous life we had learned about the great southern land and its many strange and beautiful animals. Some say that from tragedy comes opportunity. After bullying my way to the opposite coast of India, I started to listen to the streets and the slums rather than simply destroying and pillaging them. My listening led me to a man named John, who promised me, in English, that he could take me to Australia if the price was right. The price was right and I felt no need to kill him.

I boarded a tiny boat full of Indian families. There was very little room to do anything and I was tempted to make some room, using my guns and knives. I resisted, and resisted for weeks, maybe even months; a loner amongst strangers heading towards an uncertain future.

I made no friends, but more importantly, no enemies, on our voyage towards Australia. We stopped at different islands along the way, but never were we allowed to get off. Sometimes the crew stopped the boat so they could talk to people on other boats. It looked like they were asking for help and directions. They seemed very uncertain of where they needed to go and were constantly arguing and pointing out at the ocean. We had very little food and water, but just as it looked like we were about to run out, we would stop again.

After journeying for a long, long time, our boat hit something and started quickly filling up with water. As the boat began to sink, we spotted another boat on the horizon. That is when people started killing themselves by jumping into the water. They all drowned in the ocean as our vessel kept going. Soon our boat sank and we all had to swim. I was fortunate to have learned to swim in our dam at the farm in my former life, so I made it easily, while everybody else drowned.

I alone made it aboard this weird, new boat. The first thing I did was locate the kitchen to help myself to food. This was quite difficult because the kitchen was half full of ocean water.

Curiously, there was a long yellow tube that lead from the new boat down into the ocean. I used all of my strength to pull it back up as I thought it might be a fishing line. I pulled up a breathing, sleeping white man. Using all my strength and rage, I got him on board and then left him in the sun. While he was warming up, I searched around the boat for more food. I found some floating chocolate bars as well as some plastic containers full of drugs. I had come across these from time to time in my travels, but had no use for them personally. I did know, though, that with connections, drugs could be very powerful: even more powerful than a gun.

As night inevitably came, I put a blanket from a bedroom on the man. I slept near him, with my gun and my knife at the ready.

He woke up in the morning, frightened and confused.

221

Although physically healthy, his mental health was questionable.

We agreed to work together. This was the first time I had worked with anybody not at gunpoint since my days at school.

He was unlike anybody else I had ever met on my travels. His name was Kelvin. He was doing his best to concentrate between swigs of alcohol and smokes of his many different types of cigarettes. He was surely useless to me once we reached land.

The plan was simple. We were to gather our few supplies and drive the smaller boat to Australia. From there, I would kill him and steal all of his possessions. Of course, I didn't outline the last part of the plan to him.

Chapter Twenty-two

This Jendaya bird seemed to have saved my life. That made her a friend so I figured we should try to get to the mainland together. Barnes' good dory, the one that I'm sure he had made love to several times, was floating invitingly off the back of the Beche De Mer, but I could not find the keys for it anywhere. The Piece Of Shit didn't need a key. All Paul Hart, Victoria or I had to do was yank on the rip cord until our shoulders popped out, and curse at it in sweeping insults. Sometimes it took two of us doing both of those required duties at the same time to get the fucker started. But it did not require a key. If it did, I would have fuck-all chance of locating it on the semi-drowned, drug-addled and fucked-up Beche De Mer.

'Let's hit the frog and toad,' I whispered to her.

'Okay. How and why do we do that?' she replied.

'Follow me.'

The Piece Of Shit dory was also at the end of a rope out at sea. The two dories had been trailing obediently for ages. We pulled at the rope and reeled them in towards the Beche De Mer, as if the mother ship was in reverse water-labour and was reining her offspring back into her womb. We were the surgeons, assisting by pulling on the umbilical cord. Finally, and quietly, we had the POS where we wanted it, about half a metre from the edge of the mother ship.

'I'll get in if you could pass me the stuff.'

The stuff consisted of three water tanks full of petrol and my bag. I had earlier stuffed the bag full of food, clothes, snorkelling gear, water bottles, sunscreen, marijuana, pills, unidentified but certainly illegal white powder and the compass from the wheelhouse. I also had my wallet which was stuffed with the money I took out of Barnes' wallet (God rest his angry soul).

I told Jendaya to climb on board. She held on to her backpack, contents unknown. I then set about untying an impossibly huge knot that I had constructed a lifetime ago, when Barnes was alive and in charge. It took ages, and I could feel Barnes' ghostly disparagement emanating from hell.

'That's why you tie it properly the first time, you useless fuck,' a muffled, bubbling, ghostly version of Barnes's squawk said from somewhere beneath the water.

'Thanks, mate,' I whispered. 'I'll keep that in mind while I fuck another one of your nieces.'

Once the POS was untied from the Beche De Mer, I jumped ship and became captain of my new, unexpected crew of one African or Asian girl. She looked focused as she climbed aboard the dory: which made one of us. I was hoping that one of my spirit guides would come and talk to me. They didn't, so I pushed off and let the POS drift in silence away from the cocoon of the Beche De Mer.

The two of us sat in silence. Again, I was trapped on a boat with people I didn't know, including myself. I got overawed with the depth of the concept and stood there for a while, until Jendaya interrupted.

'Are we going to start the boat?'

'Yeah,' I said, 'I mean, like, really, fucking, yeah man.'

'Yes, I understand. Can we please go over the plan?'

Luckily, our plan was pretty simple and didn't require too much from me. I was going to point the POS east, and keep driving until we reached Australia. Brilliant. I guess from there we would go our separate ways.

The sea was as flat as I'd ever seen it out there. It was like a member of Bros' haircut. Occasionally, the flatness was broken by a turtle gasping for air, or a shark fin slicing through the surface. I wanted to jump in there and join them, and get away from the air but thought better of it.

I hoped that the fucking, stupid outboard motor would work for me one last fucking time. I was already pissed off at it before I tried. Angrily, I filled it up with petrol and screwed the lid on.

'All right, missus,' I yelled at it. 'You are going to work for me like the whore that you are; okay? Got it?'

My new crew watched me in casual alarm as I pulled up my imaginary sleeves and walked over to the pull cord. I grabbed onto the little, black toggle and pulled with both of my chicken arms as hard as I could.

The motor let out a brief yelp of disapproval and died.

'Fucking bitch!'

I yanked and swore harder, with the same result.

'DON'T BE AS USELESS AS A POLITICIAN; ACTUALLY DO SOMETHING, YOU MANGEY TROLLOP!'

Its response was as reserved as my plea was emphatic. Fuck.

'Jendaya, mate?' I asked.

'Yes.'

'Could you please help me try to start this bitch-slut of a cunt-whore?'

'Are you referring to the motor?'

'That's the one.'

'Well, let's start by not referring to it in derogatory female terms. It might help.'

'Okay.'

'Also, could you wipe off the petrol that you got all over it with this rag? It might help.'

'Okay.'

'And third, get out of the way and let me do it. It might help.'

I did what she told me to do. She had a voice and a vibe that I did not want to fuck with at all.

I went to the other side of the POS and sat looking wide-eyed and useless.

The sea was tranquil and expectant. The Beche De Mer had drifted out of sight. The sun was just peeking its head over the water to have a better look at the whole situation, anxious to see what had happened overnight.

Jendaya approached the outboard motor with intent. She grabbed a handful of her long, red dress (once beautiful, I'm sure) in her left mitt. She pointed her right arm outward, with her fingers stretched out pleadingly. After holding that pose for a time, she turned in a circle on the spot. Her brown eyes burned with intensity; her thoughts were not with us. Whatever space she was in, I didn't want to bump into her there.

Covering the slippery, plastic handle with the material from her dress, she slowly grabbed it with both hands and positioned her legs, ready to pull hard. She then let out the biggest primal scream possible for a being of that size as she pulled on the cord.

'KYYYYYYYYEEEEEEEEEEEEEEEEEEEAAAAAAA
AHHHHH!'

It probably woke up Australia and the Torres Strait Islands.

I ducked for cover with my hands over my ears. When I'd picked up the pieces of my shattered skull, I sat up to see Jendaya, crying in a ball, next to the running motor of HMS Piece Of Shit. It was time to go.

I grabbed the compass and headed east, as I knew it was the east coast of Australia that we wanted to get to. After cruising for half an hour, I had a quick re-think and finally concluded that we were going in the complete opposite direction of Australia. If I kept going east, I was going away from the east coast. Victoria was spot on when she had called me useless.

In hope, and trusting that my first instinct is quite often wrong, I arched the POS in a wide rainbow back toward west, trying to make it look like it was a deliberate thing, not that it seemed to matter to Jendaya. She was a crying wreck.

After a few hours, we had achieved nothing save for getting hot and dehydrated. It felt like we were in neutral in a toddler's pool, going nowhere fast, but we were (I think) getting closer to our goal of mainland Australia. The HMS Queen's Majesty Piece Of Shit was on her farewell voyage to the mainland. She bounced and skimmed and the horizon stayed distant and blue.

Then panic hit me like a dolphin tail slapping me on the chest. I'd fucked up many things before. What if I was heading the wrong way? We would surely run out of fuel soon and drift where the currents wished to take us. I'd have to eat Jendaya. I could maybe use some of her to dangle in the water, to attract sharks and turtles for food as well. But surely that would be a hit-and-miss procedure: the ocean isn't a supermarket. Or I would have to get her pregnant so that we could eat her child once every nine months.

Hmm… At least I'd get some sex out of it.

I snapped out of it. This was serious. I checked the compass. I was sure I was kind of heading west. The fuel was running out at the same rate as my sanity. There was nobody on board who I could talk to so I looked down to the ocean. The ocean had been my only friend through the whole ordeal. I wondered what the ocean would think of me. I asked it in my mind and got a response:

'You trashed a whole bunch of my coral, kidnapped and murdered my sea cucumber friends, and dumped your rubbish and bodies in me. You're going down, you reef-raper.

'You owe me, Kelvin. You dumped Jesse Barnes down here. Even in spirit form he is an absolute wanker. He won't stop squawking on about you, you and someone called Neville. You're lucky that you're alive and he's not. And those two guys you parcelled to me, the dumb-asses. Jesus Christ. They don't even realise that they're dead. They just keep beating the shit out of each other. And the boat people? Unwarranted, you tool.'

I was sure I hadn't killed any boat people.

'What about Paul Hart: has he come out of his shell a bit?' I asked the ocean, in my mind.

'Well, that's another story. I don't think you'd begin to understand his situation, and where he is. I think I've said too much already. Just know this. You'd better make this up to me big time,' it replied.

'And Victoria?'

There was no answer.

As I checked the compass, I looked up at where I was going.

'Are you okay?' asked a fierce looking Jendaya, who seemed to have recovered from her coma of woe.

'Don't be concerned. We'll be heading up the river.'

'Right.'

'Yep, pretty soon we'll be up the creek.'

'Without a paddle?'

'We don't need one.'

'No, I get the feeling that you will lead us up the creek without any assistance at all.'

Refusing to butt into any sarcasm, I took the meaning literally. So it was onward and sort of westward, towards the land of beer, bogans, and the Brisbane Broncos.

Jendaya gestured towards the horizon.

'Land, there's land. We've found mother-fucking land!' I yelled.

'Well done, Kelvin,' said Jendaya.

'Thank you,' I replied.

'I honestly thought that, having fought all this time to get here, I was going to die alongside you before ever seeing Australia.'

'Well, your confidence in me has paid off. Although, fuck-knows what we are going to do when we get there.'

'Kelvin, do you have a gun?'

'No, Jendaya, do you?'

'No,' she said quickly.

'So, what do we do now?'

Just as we reached the mouth of a river, our brave little dory finally chugged out of petrol, leaving us drifting. We stared out into the mangroves flanking us. Storm clouds brewed overhead.

Missives Of Merpeople

Dear Father,

I am a being of honour. It is for that reason I cannot return to the ocean depths. My loyalty cannot be to the sect, or to you, or even to myself any longer. My life has been saved by a land dweller and threatened by another merperson.

During my final boat assignment, our commander's life was terminated by the ocean and its creatures. As a result, the rest of my pod had access to many substances that were forbidden to us previously. Upon taking them, I experienced an unusual arrangement of thoughts, feelings, and emotions. I think I even found my 'sense of humour.'

Unfortunately, the experience left me paralysed. I lay still for hours and hours, until my lungs and heart became dormant and my inner gills very nearly dried up. When I had lost all hope, the pod member known as Kelvin arrived. He somehow realised the urgency of my situation, and threw me into the life-giving ocean. His loving gesture saved my life, although it was too late for two of my fallen pod members.

As I floated in the water, recuperating, I was attacked by a merwoman. I hadn't come across another of my kind for some time. She submerged from aboard the

Beche De Mer. I instantly recognised her as the one they called Victoria in the world of the land dwellers. She had been deceiving me and the others all this time, yet I do not know why. I also do not know why she was trying to kill me.

Her poisonous spines emerged from her back and her shoulders. She had bigger, sharper teeth than I had seen on anything in the ocean before. I was very lucky to avoid her first attack. I managed to swerve away from her on pure instinct. This act of defiance seemed to make her angry, and she hurtled towards me at full pace, teeth first. I responded by swimming away as fast as I could, tail turned. I had reverted to full merman form, and also had my spines out. It became apparent that my assailant would catch me soon if I failed to take action, so I stopped suddenly, back-spines rigid and elongated. It worked: my assailant lanced herself all over my back, piercing her head, chest, stomach and gills. She was motionless immediately, and she sank to the depths.

I got lucky. I hope no more are sent.

The whole ordeal left me confused and shaken and it took me days to locate my saviour. He is in a small vessel heading towards the mainland with an unknown woman.

He does not realise that the area they are headed for is home to many crocodiles, so I must stay close, submerged, to ward off danger.

I recently sensed him communicating directly with the ocean, a power I have not encountered in anybody except the most learned of Mermen. His environmental sensitivity and compassion may one day be of great importance to us.

I have also found many strange messages left within the kelp and the seaweed in this area. The imprints are very strong. They tell a tale, a tale I shall share:

An age ago, the land dwellers and the merpeople were friends. They lived in harmony together.

The merpeople offered treasures from the sea to the land dwellers.

The land dwellers offered treasures from the land to the merpeople.

The merpeople allowed the land dwellers access to the oceans: they encouraged them and taught them to swim.

The land dwellers allowed merpeople access to the land: they encouraged them and taught them to walk.

The land dwellers became very strong swimmers, and the merpeople became very strong walkers.

'We shall take this land, for we can now walk. We shall have all of the treasures that the world has to offer,' proclaimed the merpeople.

'We are not offering our land to you,' replied the land dwellers.

'Then we will fight a war and you shall not win,' proclaimed the merpeople.

'It is not our choice to fight, but we must defend ourselves,' said the land dwellers.

'Our oceans and your land shall be ruled by the merpeople,' they proclaimed.

A terrible war raged for years and years. Treasures from both land and sea were used to make weapons. Eventually, the land dwellers surrendered, as most of their numbers were slaughtered.

'The land now belongs to the merpeople. You shall be our slaves,' said the merpeople.

The merpeople roamed the land, using the land dwellers for labour. They had all of the treasures from both the sea and the land. The land dwellers began to die rapidly until there was only one left.

'Please remember our time of harmony. Remember an age when we would swim in your ocean and you would walk on our land. Remember me,' said the last

land dweller, as he died under the whip of the merpeople.

The merpeople had learned much from the land dwellers before they destroyed them. They built houses and cities and settled on the land. They no longer needed to swim in the ocean. Soon, all but very few of the merpeople moved out of the ocean to live on the land. They built cities and aeroplanes. They fought wars between themselves. They built enormous boats to empty the sea of all of its treasures. They forgot who they were.

The merpeople who stayed in the ocean became wary of their land-dwelling relatives and resided only in the deepest depths.

The story continues so to this day.

The mangroves in which I lurk are infested with messages of our past, as well as crocodiles. I feel that a great battle took place here.

This tale is vitally important. The message is very strong. It says that we are the descendants of the humans whom we avoid and abhor so much. I shall find out more.

Out of honour for my saviour, the sect and to the merpeople, I must not return until my work is done.

And so it is that I stay alert, but submerged, by my saviour's vessel, should he ever need help.

Honour and love for my race always,

Your Son.

Dear Son,

It is clear that your mind is made up and I shall no longer try to persuade you home through any means. Your mother is proud, as am I.

Your Father.

Chapter Twenty-three

Jendaya reached into her backpack and produced a big, black, shiny handgun.

'You said that you didn't have one of those,' I stated.

'Well I lied,' she said.

'Well fucking duh,' I shot back.

'I want you to get off the boat, and then I am going to steal all of your things and then I am going to kill you,' she said with abrupt honesty.

I was perfectly happy not too long before to keep diving deeper and deeper into the ocean until eternity began, but now I was not so thrilled about the idea of death.

'Jendaya, champ,' I said bravely, 'I don't think that killing me is a great idea. Don't shoot me yet. I can still help you. This is my country, you know. I can help you survive and prosper here,' I pleaded.

She looked at me with some interest, so I kept pressing the point home.

'You are a foreign-looking girl in the middle of the rainforest. There will be no blending in for you.'

I thought I was getting somewhere.

'Besides,' I continued, 'we are mates, aren't we. You wouldn't kill a friend, would you?'

'Enough!' she interrupted. 'I see your point, Kelvin. Let us both get off this tiny little boat. You first,' she said, with the weapon still pointed at me.

Jendaya followed me onto the muddy bank and with impressive strength she hauled the boat onto the river's edge, making sure that the gun was always pointed at my chest.

There was a cold menace in her eyes.

'Well, fuck. Fuck this shit. I am finally back on land and now I am going to die,' I thought out loud. 'Could you please let me wash down all of these drugs with alcohol and let me freak out in the forest first?'

'No,' she said, making a clicky sound on the gun.

I couldn't believe that this shit was going down the way it was. Jendaya had completely lost it, or second-guessed me, or something. Maybe I had lost it a long time ago, and she had just realised how dangerous I was. Either way, she held the power.

I decided it was time to use my lady-magic on her.

'Do you fancy a fuck before you kill me?' I asked, pleadingly. It didn't work. It actually seemed to make her angrier, but in a contained way, like a muzzled pit-bull.

'You would be wise not to proposition me,' she said, almost courteously.

'What, otherwise you'll kill me more?' I chimed back.

'But seriously, Jendaya. I wasn't really propositioning you. I was just trying to buy some time. I am a nice bloke and I am just trying not to die. And if you stick with me I can help you to not die too.'

She pondered that, long and hard. I saw uncertainty in her eyes for a brief second, so I seized on it.

'Do you know anybody in this country? Do you know anything about the wildlife here? The only thing you know is me, and I can help you. I can help you get money from the government. I can help you find your feet.

'I have no idea where you are from or what your past is. All I know is that I can't help you if you kill me.'

She remained still, her eyes firmly on me, her gun still pointed directly at me.

'Come on, Jendaya,' I said, encouragingly. 'Put the gun down and we can grab a coffee and work out what to do next.'

She smiled and relaxed. She lowered her gun ever so slightly, so it was pointing more towards my stomach than my chest.

A creature sprang at Jendaya from the murky river. It was roughly man-shaped and man-sized, but was covered in green goo and had long gill slits on either side of its body. It had big sharp spines sticking out of its back.

Jendaya, undaunted, shot several rounds into the beast, which shrieked grotesquely and fell back into the water with a huge splash. She continued to shoot at the river until the splashing stopped, then trained the gun back on me.

'See, I told you you'd have to watch out for the wildlife. This is why you need a local guide. 'I think it would be best if we take a few steps away from the river. I was going to tell you that before, but I was too busy talking you out of killing me,' I said.

My head rang with the sound of shooting. Jendaya lowered her gun and walked towards me. The storm-clouds opened and it suddenly pissed with tropical rain.

'We need to find shelter. I can help you, Jendaya.'

Missives Of Merpeople: Final Missive

Dear Father,

I urgently need help. I have hopefully repaid my debt to the land dweller Kelvin Daniels. He was nearly attacked by one of his own species, a common occurrence above the water.

I distracted the assailant into firing her ammunition at me. I am now in mortal peril, as I know that only time in the water can heal my multiple wounds. The crocodiles and sharks of the mangroves shall surely soon become aware of my weakened mental and physical state. I hope that my thoughts are strong enough to imprint on the currents. I require assistance and I know, father, that you can help me.

If I do not survive, please tell Merpeople far and wide the story of our beginnings.

Your Ever Loyal and Loving Son

###

CPSIA information can be obtained at www.ICGtesting.com
Printed in the USA
BVOW011552080713

325352BV00011B/395/P

9 781463 775834